"Would you like some more?" asked Derek

Candice shook her head and leaned away from the sparkling dinner table. "Wish I could."

"So?"

"What?" She feigned confusion, hoping that he'd forgotten their bet of a kiss for every point out of ten that he earned with this meal.

"How many points are we talking?" He cocked an eyebrow and grinned.

"I could...give you a zero."

"You could." He gazed at her knowingly.

"Oh, man." Candice closed her eyes and raised a hand to her forehead. She couldn't believe she was about to do this. Her nemesis, her archrival, and she was going to have to...pay him a *compliment*, not to mention—

"Zero to ten," Derek said softly.

"Ten," she whispered, and puckered her lips.

R

Note from the editor...

An Evening To Remember... Those words evoke all kinds of emotions and memories. How do you plan a romantic evening with your guy that will help you get in touch with each other on every level?

Start with a great dinner that you cook together. Be sure to light several candles and put fresh flowers on the table. Enjoy a few glasses of wine and pick out your favorite music to set the mood. After dinner take the time to really talk to each other. Hold hands and snuggle on the sofa in front of the fireplace. And maybe take a few minutes to read aloud selected sexy scenes from your favorite Harlequin Temptation novel. After that, anything can happen....

That's just one way to have an evening to remember. There are so many more. Write and tell us how you keep the spark in your relationship. And don't forget to check out our Web site at www.eHarlequin.com.

Sincerely,
Birgit Davis-Todd
Executive Editor

BARBARA DUNLOP

HIGH STAKES

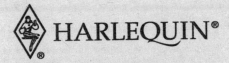

TORONTO • NEW YORK • LONDON
AMSTERDAM • PARIS • SYDNEY • HAMBURG
STOCKHOLM • ATHENS • TOKYO • MILAN • MADRID
PRAGUE • WARSAW • BUDAPEST • AUCKLAND

ISBN 0-373-69210-2

HIGH STAKES

Copyright © 2005 by Barbara Dunlop.

This edition published by arrangement with Harlequin Books S.A.

® and TM are trademarks of the publisher. Trademarks indicated with
® are registered in the United States Patent and Trademark Office, the
Canadian Trade Marks Office and in other countries.

www.eHarlequin.com

Printed in U.S.A.

Dear Reader,

Here's the final story of the Reeves-DuCarter brothers. From the moment brother Derek appeared in *Next to Nothing!* to give his baby brother hell and his middle brother sage advice in *Flying High,* I've known that when Derek's turn came, he was going to fall fast and he was going to fall hard.

Sure enough, Candice Hammond, the daughter of his archenemy, rocked Derek's world. He's used to being in charge, yet she challenges him at every turn. The woman is his intellectual and emotional match, and she's going toe to toe with the millionaire entrepreneur until he gives her everything she wants. Which is also everything he wants, though he doesn't know it yet.

I truly hope you enjoy the Reeves-DuCarter brothers. They've been a delight for me to live with and I'm thrilled to be able to share them. I'd love to hear from you at www.barbaradunlop.com.

Best,

Barbara Dunlop

Books by Barbara Dunlop

*Tall, Dark & Restless

To Dad.
With appreciation, admiration and love.

1

"YOU'RE ALWAYS THE BEST MAN, but never the groom...." Derek Reeves's brother Tyler propped his elbows on the terrace guardrail outside the ballroom of the Quayside Hotel. Orchestra music and muted laughter from their middle brother, Striker's, wedding reception wafted through the open French doors into the clear September night.

Derek grinned to himself. He'd admit to feeling a little smug about being the Reeves family's sole remaining bachelor. He turned his back on the rose garden, the marble fountain and Lake Washington and imitated his brother's pose. "Jealous?" he asked.

Tyler's gaze strayed through the open doors to where Jenna, his wife of three months, chatted with the other bridesmaids. There was a thread of incredulous laughter in his voice. "Not hardly."

Derek took a swig of his ice water. He had to admit that Jenna was great. So was Erin, Striker's new bride. But they were still wives. They had needs, demands and agendas. Derek was planning to be his own man for a long time to come.

Tyler nodded at the water. "You the designated driver or something?"

Derek shook his head. "I'm expecting a call from Tokyo."

"You brought your cell phone to your brother's *wedding?*"

"I turned it off during the ceremony."

"We have *got* to get you a life."

"By life, I'm assuming you mean a ball and chain of my own? Misery may love company, little brother, but I don't think so."

Tyler raised his glass of Scotch in a mock toast. "Come on in, the water's fine."

The wind picked up off the lake, bringing with it the scent of roses, as Derek slid his brother a skeptical gaze. "Uh-huh."

"I'm serious."

"I'm *perfectly* happy on my own."

"How do you know?"

Derek frowned. "What kind of a question is that?"

"When's the last time you had a steady girlfriend?"

"Define steady."

"Longer than eight hours."

The frown turned to another grin. It *had* been a while. Which meant Derek's life was ticking along exactly the way he liked it. "Few months. Maybe a year."

"We need to find you a nice girl to bring home to Mom."

Derek let out a chopped laugh at the sappy expression on Tyler's face. "There's nothing worse than a reformed bachelor."

"Hey, I'm being serious here."

"So am I. If I want a woman, I'll find a woman. No offense, bro, but I don't need your help on the romance front."

Tyler snorted. "Romance? I think they're called one-night stands."

"And your point is…"

"My point is, you're hanging out with the wrong kind of women."

"Well, the right kind of woman sure isn't going to hang out with me."

Derek had been in Europe three times this month. He had to be in Japan on the fifth. And if he didn't figure out a way to salvage that electronics deal they'd just lost to Hammond Electronics, he'd be drumming up wireless business in rural Brazil. He somehow suspected most nice girls would insist he spend at least half his life on the North American continent.

"You never know," said Tyler, making a show of sizing Derek up. "They *might* be able to get past your looks."

"Nice try, pretty boy."

Tyler laughed.

"The rest of you shareholders should be grateful I've stayed single."

"Why?"

"The minute I have a little woman at home, the bottom line's going to suffer."

Tyler clicked his teeth, shook his head and gave Derek a pitying look.

"Don't get sarcastic with me," said Derek. "Women dilute a man's focus. They want him to cater to their little whims, bring home presents, talk about their feelings."

"Not all women are like that. Jenna's not like that."

"Yeah? When's the last time you two spent an evening apart?"

Tyler glanced toward the ballroom again.

"A week?" asked Derek. "A month? Anytime since the wedding?"

"It's not because I can't—"

"Right," Derek drawled, knowing he'd easily won the round. Time to move the conversation along. "So while you were busy cuddling and whispering sweet nothings, did Jenna happen to say anything about the Lighthouse renovations?"

The Lighthouse Restaurant was a showpiece on the top floor of the family-owned Quayside Hotel. It was being renovated by Jenna and Candice Hammond's company, Canna Interiors.

"She says you and Candice have been fighting again," said Tyler.

"How could I fight with Candice? I've been in London for the past three days."

"Candice obviously didn't notice you were gone. She kept right on fighting."

"Only way she can win," Derek muttered.

"You do realize that you two are driving Jenna nuts."

"So get Jenna to talk to Candice." It wasn't Derek's fault that Candice was impossible.

"Candice says you're micromanaging."

Like hell. "I'm making sure Candice Hammond doesn't blow three and a half million of my dollars."

"They're a reputable company."

"She's out for revenge."

"Why?"

"Because you and I *lied* to them."

"Jenna and I are happily married. Candice isn't mad anymore."

"She may not be mad at you, but she's still plotting against me."

"You're paranoid."

Derek took another swallow of his water. Paranoia was a highly underrated quality in a corporate executive. It had saved Derek's ass more than once. "Just because I'm paranoid, doesn't mean she's not out to get me."

"GET IT, CANDICE!" cried Jenna as Erin tossed the bridal bouquet over her head toward the middle of the Quayside ballroom.

Candice cringed when she realized it was coming in her direction. She faded to the back of the pack, vowing to *thank* Jenna later for calling even more attention to her single, relationship-less, dateless status. Cream-colored roses and pale orchids arced gracefully toward the domed ceiling, far above the heads of young women who'd gathered in a cluster.

That Erin had some arm on her.

Candice took another step back, then another and another. The women in front of her stretched up, their fingertips just missing the ribbon streamers as the bouquet's trajectory brought it back toward earth.

They were all missing, turning, frowning…

Candice's eyes widened in disbelief. Who would have thought Erin could toss that puppy thirty-five feet? Despite her efforts to avoid it, the huge bouquet zeroed in on her like radar. It plunked against her chest, and her arms automatically went around it.

Jenna dashed over from the sidelines, cheering madly in her apricot bridesmaid dress and high heels. Tiny sprigs of baby's breath jiggled in her upswept hair. "Great catch," she sang.

"Gee, thanks."

Jenna laughed. "Now all we need to do is find you a man."

Candice quickly shifted the bouquet to one hand, lowering it and tucking it behind her thigh, trying to shake the feeling that all eyes in the room were on her. Why didn't somebody just write up a big Loser sign and paste it to her forehead?

It wasn't that she had any particular interest in getting married. It was more that the world at large seemed to think twenty-seven was too old to be single. Like she was some kind of wrinkled spinster.

Jenna scanned the room. "Let's see. Not too tall. Somebody with good career prospects. We want patience and a good sense of humor, since you can be—" She abruptly snapped her mouth shut.

"Since I can be *what*?" asked Candice, eyeing up her friend and business partner. Even wearing a satin gown and baby's breath, Jenna still managed to look calculating.

Jenna didn't answer.

"Are you suggesting I'm grumpy?" asked Candice.

"Testy."

"*Testy?*"

The single men lined up for the garter toss, and Jenna took Candice by the arm, pulling her aside. "Only sometimes."

Candice was more than happy to vacate center stage. She looked around for a nearby table to abandon the bouquet. If she was lucky, one of the eager, single ladies would steal it. "I'm never testy," she said.

Jenna patted her arm. "I'm thinking about you and Derek."

Candice rolled her eyes at the mention of Derek's name. She and Jenna had been working on the Lighthouse Restaurant renovation for three months now, and he'd been her shadow—like she couldn't be trusted. Well, she had news for him. *He'd* lied to *her*, not the other way around.

"He's the testy one," she said to Jenna.

"Only when you're around."

Oh, sure, like it was Candice's fault. "He's arrogant, overbearing, bossy and conceited."

Jenna smiled. "Yeah. But in a good way."

A roar rose from the crowd of men as Erin's garter sailed through the air. A hand shot up and snagged it. The successful man let out a whoop and made a big show of twirling it around his index finger. At least somebody was happy about being publicly tagged as *next*.

Jenna tilted her head and checked out the garter catcher. "Maybe you just need to get laid."

Candice wasn't sure she'd heard right. "Excuse me?"

"After three months of marriage, I can highly recommend it."

"Over-sharing," said Candice.

Jenna grinned, nodding toward the group of men. "I bet any one of them would be willing—"

Candice took a backward step. "Think I'll go up and check on the Lighthouse."

"What's to check? You're off duty, and we're setting you up here."

There was no way in the world Candice was hanging around while Jenna *set her up*. She tried to pull her arm from Jenna's grasp. "I want to make sure the paneling was delivered."

Jenna's hand tightened. "It's not like you'll be able to do anything about it before Monday."

Candice reached out to disentangle Jenna's fingers. "I'll sleep better if I take a quick look. You go ahead and scope out prospects while I'm gone."

Jenna brightened. "Really?"

"Sure. Why not?" Since Candice had no intention

of coming back to the wedding reception, Jenna could scope to her heart's content. Candice wasn't even planning to go up to the restaurant. Just as soon as she was out of sight, she was heading for the main door of the lobby and grabbing a taxi.

"See you later." She started in the direction of the express elevator that serviced the rooftop restaurant. As she walked, she kept an eye on Jenna to gauge the best moment for her escape.

Not quite yet. Tyler had appeared out of the crowd, and both he and Jenna focused on Candice. They exchanged a few words, and then Tyler's eyes lit up. They both waved happily.

Jenna had obviously enlisted his aid. How humiliating.

Candice gave them a brittle smile and waved back, making a show of pressing the elevator button. Unfortunately, the elevator was parked on the ballroom floor, and the doors immediately opened. She had no choice but to step inside.

Then the doors slid shut behind her, blocking out the orchestra and the buzz of conversation. She sighed in relief as she leaned against the cool wall, resting her hands on the metal rail, tipping her head back. It was nice in here.

The elevator rushed smoothly upward. Through the outer glass wall, Candice could see the black lake, the stars and the lights of Seattle.

She loved the Quayside. As the major shareholder, Derek was a major pain, but the building was beau-

tiful. It was a stunning example of mid-twentieth
century red brick and terra-cotta.

She and Jenna's decorating business, Canna Interiors, was just getting established in Seattle, so they
were taking every job they were offered. But Candice
hoped they'd be able to specialize in historic buildings like the Quayside. They were the city's heart
and soul.

The doors slid open on the fortieth floor, and she
decided she'd better kill a little time before going
back down to escape. She left the elevator, and her
footsteps echoed on the raw plywood as she made
her way down the hall.

The entire floor was closed for renovation. The
paneling had been delivered, but then she'd already
known that. Sheets of plywood, stacks of wood paneling and cans of paint were clustered against the
foyer walls.

She passed through the big, antique double doors
that led into the dining room. The wallboard had
been peeled back to reveal arched window openings,
and the glaziers had just finished installing new windows. The view of the city was spectacular.

Abandoning the bouquet on a sawhorse, she
squinted around the room, picturing antique light
fixtures, turn-of-the-century paintings, white tablecloths, hurricane lamps and fine china. Her gaze
caught and held on the half-finished wine rack, ap-
prehension sliding through her stomach. Something
wasn't right.

She started toward it.

Lifting the plans from the raw wood top, she read the hand-scrawled note stapled to one corner. She stifled the urge to scream. She'd given specific instructions on the placement and the dimensions of the wine rack. But Derek had undermined her authority, yet again.

She crumpled the note in a tight fist. He might be the reason she and Jenna had this job in the first place, but she had to put a stop to the man's meddling. Forget cutting out on the reception, maybe she'd go back to the ballroom and track him down. Track him down, corner him and set the ground rules once and for all.

As she formulated a scathing lecture, the elevator doors down the hall whirred open. Measured, masculine footsteps headed along the passageway toward her. Perfect. Jenna had sent up a date. Could the evening get any worse?

She started toward the double doors, intent on sending the hapless man away. But when Derek appeared, she stopped short.

Tall, broad-shouldered and athletic, his strong chin, aristocratic nose and piercing blue eyes combined with his wealth and power to give him anything he wanted in life.

But not this time.

Not with her.

He froze, hitting her with a narrow-eyed, suspicious gaze. "What are *you* doing up here?"

"At the moment, I'm trying to figure out how much damage you've done."

He continued toward her, imposing in his best man tux. "What are you talking about? What damage?"

As he grew closer, she was glad to be wearing three-inch heels.

Drawing herself up, refusing to be intimidated, she folded her arms across her chest and nodded at the wine rack. "Take a look at that."

Before focusing on the wine rack, Derek's gaze stopped for a moment on the empty doorway, a puzzled frown forming on his face. Then he moved on. "I don't see any damage."

The muscles in the back of her neck tensed, and her voice went up an octave. "Of course you don't. Because you have no *clue* what we're doing here."

"I know exactly what we're doing here. We're renovating *my* restaurant."

Candice stepped closer to the wine rack, gesturing to the base with an open hand. "Are you *trying* to waste money?"

"I'm trying to save money."

"False economy."

Derek's full mouth curved up in a cynical grin. "How many millions do you suppose have been wasted using that logic?"

"You have trust issues, you know that?"

"I trust people."

"Uh-huh."

"As long as they're within my sight."

Candice pointed at him and then pointed to her chest. "*You* lied to *me*, remember?"

"And you threatened to waste my money."

"Because you'd told us you were Derek Reeves—"

"I *am* Derek Reeves."

"Being Derek Reeves is quite different than being Derek Reeves-DuCarter."

"You never fessed up to being Candice Hammond, either."

Candice had to admit, it was odd they'd gone two weeks without realizing each other's identity. She'd heard about the Reeves-DuCarters all her life, had known they were in competition with her father, had even met Derek's father at a party or two. Still, she hadn't put it together.

"I never lied about who I was," she said.

"No," Derek agreed. "It was Tyler that kept that little tidbit to himself."

"So pick on your brother, and leave me alone."

"I can't leave you alone."

"Why not?"

"Because you're mad enough to waste my money."

"I'm also professional enough to fix your mistakes."

Derek shook his head, coughing out a cold laugh.

Candice shimmied into a crouch position, pointing to the base of the wine rack to prove her point. "You know the marble top's precut?"

He crouched beside her. "So?"

"So, exhibit A, *you* had them build the base two

feet off. That's false economy, because we're going to have to rip it out and start over again."

"That's faulty logic. Because I just moved the wine rack. I didn't change the dimensions."

"If you'd bothered to read the plans, you'd know we have to recess it into the wall."

"I did bother to read the plans. They told me you wanted to rebuild an entire wall for the sake of two feet."

She raised her eyebrows. There was a master plan at work here. Details mattered. Something Derek obviously didn't grasp. "Your point is?"

He straightened and held out his hand. "You're scary, you know that?"

She ignored his unspoken offer. But halfway up, her toe caught on the hem of her dress and she stumbled. He caught her arm to steady her.

The feel of his calluses against her skin sent an instant shock wave through her body. She gritted her teeth against the sensation. "You're the scary one." What with his drive-by style of executive interference, and…

She shook off his hand.

"Because I catch you when you fall?" His deep voice rumbled close to her ear.

She took a quick step away from him, remembering the last time he'd touched her, spoken to her in that vibrating, intimate tone that made her blood dance. It was three months ago, on that silly carnival ride, the Tunnel of Love. It was the day she found out he was a fraud. The day they'd found out Tyler was spying on Jenna.

She shook off the memory, rubbing his touch away from her bare arm. "Do you want a five-star restaurant or a diner?"

"Oh, definitely a diner," he drawled, cocking his head sideways.

"Well, you're well on your way."

"You are so melodramatic."

"You are so naive."

His eyes widened at that one.

She began counting off on her fingertips. "We have an artist on retainer. We've consulted on the marble pattern. We've already bought paintings for the recessed wall. The lines on the marble will flow perfectly toward the pillars, emphasize the mini atrium and the windows—"

"*You* may have a heady, artistic vision, but *I* have an obligation to the other shareholders."

"To ruin the renovation?"

"To make sure Reeves-DuCarter worldwide share prices don't plummet when the financial markets hear how much you're spending on a wine rack."

"It's the focal point of the entire room—"

"Hey, Derek."

Candice clamped her mouth shut and drew back at the sound of Tyler Reeves's voice.

"There you are," said Derek. "I thought you'd died in the hallway."

"Can I borrow your cell phone?" asked Tyler.

Candice glanced from man to man. Both were tall and broad shouldered, with short dark hair and those startling blue eyes. Tyler was slightly slimmer, and he always looked a whole lot happier.

"Did the reception move up here?" she asked.

It was one thing for her to duck out on Erin and Striker. She was just another wedding guest. But Derek and Tyler were in their brother's wedding party.

"I just need to check on something," said Tyler, holding out his hand for the phone.

Derek looked confused, but he reached into the pocket of his tux jacket. "Yeah… Sure…"

"Thanks," Tyler nodded, taking Derek's phone and heading back out the door.

"No problem," said Derek.

Candice wondered why Tyler hadn't used a house phone downstairs. There had to be a hundred of them.

While she puzzled over his presence, he paused in the doorway. Then turned back to face them, tapping the phone against the bottom of his chin. His expression shifted from affable to stern.

"You two are upsetting my wife," he said.

"Upsetting Jenna?" asked Candice, instantly worried. Jenna had been fine when she'd left her ten minutes ago. It couldn't be *that* important to her that Candice get a date.

Tyler reached for the two doors. "And I've decided you need some time alone together to work things out." He quickly pulled the doors shut and clicked the dead bolt into place.

"What the hell?" Derek was at the doors in three long strides. "Tyler? My phone!"

"Jenna suggested a time-out," came Tyler's muffled voice from the other side of the solid oak.

"Time-out from what?" called Derek.

"Like in kindergarten. You two kids see about settling your differences before the crew shows up on Monday."

2

SETTLE THEIR *DIFFERENCES*? Candice darted a glance at Derek's rock-hard jaw and narrowed eyes. "What does he mean *Monday?*"

Derek's lips thinned, but he didn't answer.

She quickly turned her attention to the dead bolt. It was keyed from both sides, and she didn't have a key.

Tyler had *locked* them in the restaurant.

"Tyler?" she asked hopefully, moving up against the oak, testing the knob. "Uh, Tyler?"

No reply.

Derek let out an exasperated curse. "I don't think he's out there."

"He'll be back," she said, nodding confidently, stepping back and gazing up at the oversized doors. "This has to be a joke."

"I didn't hear Tyler laughing."

"Jenna won't let him leave us here."

"What makes you think he'll tell Jenna?"

"Well… Because…" Candice hated to admit it, but that was a good question.

Brushing past her, Derek tested the knob, then he rattled the doors. "I sincerely doubt he'll tell her."

"She's his *wife*. Isn't there something in the wedding vows about honesty?"

Derek stepped back beside her to survey the doors. He let out a hard sigh, shaking his head in pity, voice dropping to that intimate timbre. "Candy, Candy, Candy—"

"I asked you not to call me that."

"Tyler thinks he's saving Jenna."

"Well, that would be *your* fault."

Derek held up his hands in a gesture of surrender. "How is it *my* fault?"

"Jenna's frustrated, because you keep picking fights, undermining my instructions—"

"I do have veto power."

"Over the stain color? The wainscoting? The positioning of the wine rack?" If Derek would just let her do her job, they wouldn't be in this fix. She was really quite easy to get along with.

"Over any little thing I want," he said.

"You have taken things way beyond the spirit of the contract."

"Your threatening to bankrupt me takes things beyond the spirit of the contract."

"I did not threaten bankrupting you." Candice folded her arms across her chest. "I am a professional."

He gave a dry chuckle. "You said, and I quote, 'I have a contract for three-point-five million of your dollars, and I intend to spend every cent.'"

Candice shifted uncomfortably. "I was upset." It hadn't been the most professional moment of her career. But, Derek *did* that to her.

He ran his fingers around the seams of the doors. "The true measure of a professional isn't what she does when things are going *well*."

"You don't think you and Tyler lying to us, conspiring against us, hiding your identities amounts to extraordinary circumstances."

"Tyler was working undercover."

"Tyler was also sleeping with Jenna."

"She seems to have forgiven him."

"He deserved to be forgiven."

Derek stared at her in silence for a moment. "Unlike me."

"You're still a problem, Derek."

"We're still locked in a restaurant, Candy."

"It's Candice."

He grinned.

"Okay, fine. You're right. Let's table it for now."

He nodded in agreement. "We can always pick up the fight after we're free."

She nodded in return. "Deal. So, did you bring your master key?"

"Won't fit this lock."

"It's a *master* key."

"The door and the lock are old. And unique. We haven't locked it in years."

Candice eyed the carved oak slabs. "You think you could break it down?"

"It's solid oak. Besides, isn't it pivotal to the flow of the room or something?"

"True." It was a feature she'd planned to use. They'd refinish it, replace the brass. Maybe change the lock in case this kind of thing ever happened again.

It would be a shame to break it. But she was starting to feel claustrophobic. Not that the room was small. In fact, it was huge. It was just that Derek took up so darn much of it.

Suddenly, inspiration hit. *The kitchen.* She headed across the dining room. "There's a door through the kitchen."

"Blocked by the new refrigeration unit," Derek called after her.

"We should at least check it out."

"Waste of time," he said, but he followed.

"Pessimist," she countered.

"Realist," he corrected.

"Cynic." She stopped in front of the crated refrigeration unit. It was huge. She suspected even former linebacker Derek wouldn't be able to budge this thing.

"Jenna will be here soon," Candice said with more confidence than she felt.

"Maybe."

"I'm sure she'll notice we're missing."

"She's probably got her mind on her Tyler right now. I hear weddings make women feel romantic."

Candice had to admit, Derek had a point. For some women. "Not me."

"Why does that not surprise me?"

Candice lined her hands up against the rough wooden crate and pushed as hard as she could. "I am *not* staying in here until Monday. I have things to do, places to go." She had the library redecorating proposal to finish this weekend. The deadline was Wednesday and there were still a hundred details to check.

"Are you hinting that I don't?"

"Well you're not acting like it." She pushed harder. For a big-time international conglomerate executive, he seemed pretty blasé about losing a huge chunk of his time.

"Candy—"

"Don't call me that."

Derek leaned back against a butcher's block. "It weighs a ton."

She glared at him as she peeled off her high heels. "Wimp."

He straightened and opened one of the drawers under the counter, pawing through the contents. "I'm speaking literally. It weighs two thousand pounds. Sometimes you have to accept defeat."

"How'd you ever get to be a millionaire with an attitude like that?" She turned her back on the crate and tried pushing it butt first.

"How do you manage to keep clients with an attitude like yours?"

"I'm an extremely reasonable person."

"You're trying to push a two thousand pound refrigeration unit in your stocking feet."

She clamped her jaw on a small smile and stopped pushing. "That's not unreasonable."

He held up a carving knife, flexing the blade. "You weigh what, a hundred? It defies at least one law of physics."

She eyed the sharp edge. "Have I annoyed you that badly?"

He frowned and tossed the knife back into the drawer. "None of these will work on countersunk screws. We may be stuck."

"How stuck?"

"Real stuck."

"As in you and me? All night long?"

He shot her a look that sizzled right down to her toes. "Candy—"

"Don't call me that."

"Don't leave yourself wide-open like that."

Raw energy pulsed between them for a long second. Candice felt her skin prickle and her heart rate speed up. She was suddenly short of breath.

"Derek?"

"Yeah?"

"We have *got* to get out of here."

Now that was an understatement. Never mind the fact that Derek had piles of work waiting on his desk, or the fact that Ray Yamamoto was about to have a cell phone conversation with Tyler, Derek and Candice were inches short of combusting at the best of times. Leave them alone for thirty-six hours and anything could happen.

She was drop-dead gorgeous in that tight purple dress. Despite himself, it wasn't the first time he'd felt an attraction to her. She was smart. And she was feisty. And she made him stop and think, and feel, and want....

Spending the night alone together was foolish at best, suicidal at worst.

"I'll go look for some tools," he said, determined to exhaust every possibility before giving in.

"Tools?" She stepped back from the crate, her stocking-covered feet slipping against the tiled kitchen floor.

"Maybe we can take the door off the hinges," he elaborated.

Her green eyes brightened in surprise. "That's a good idea."

"A compliment, Candy?"

She frowned again at the nickname, but didn't correct him this time. "Don't let it go to your head."

Derek chuckled as he headed back into the dining room. Candy was definitely a misnomer, given her tart personality. But he got a kick out of the way the name made her bristle.

He glanced around the dining room. Plywood, two-by-fours and sheets of foam insulation were stacked against the walls. The floor was littered with sawdust and shavings. And the dining tables were clustered in one corner, protected by a canvas tarpaulin.

The carpenters were half done, the plumbers had moved in last week, and the electricians had cut holes in everything that didn't move.

Although it looked like the tools had been cleaned up for the weekend, Derek was hoping somebody had left something behind. He headed toward the new bank of windows overlooking the hotel board-walk and the marina on Lake Washington. He'd definitely give Jenna and Candice points for discovering the big arched window openings. The view alone was going to increase the Lighthouse's customer base.

He peeked under a couple of tarps and moved some plywood, hoping for an air ratchet or a stray Phillips head screwdriver. He found nothing. The tradesmen were obviously neat and well organized.

"Any luck?" asked Candice from the kitchen doorway. She'd left her shoes behind.

He wasn't sure which was worse, the way her sleek little calves had curved down toward the skinny straps and spiky heels, or her sexy stocking-clad feet. The strapless dress revealed her smooth shoulders, and it was tight enough to prove that, despite the hard edge to her arguments, she had a body that was soft in all the right places.

Her blond hair was done up in swirls and curls, but the long evening was beginning to show on it. Wisps had worked their way free to tickle her temples and the base of her neck. She oozed tousled sensuality, and he had to drag his attention away.

"Nothing so far," he said.

She began hunting from the other end of the room. "Why would Tyler do something this drastic?"

"He's protecting Jenna." Derek was trying to be charitable toward his brother, but he had to admit it was tough to keep from plotting his demise.

"He doesn't need to protect Jenna from me. I'm her partner, her friend. I was her maid of honor for goodness' sake."

He lifted the last tarp, checking a makeshift construction table underneath. Sawdust, a measuring tape, a plumb line and a carpenter's pencil. Nothing of any value to their current plight. "It's your relationship with me that's the problem."

Candice stepped carefully around a couple of sawhorses. "I don't have a relationship with you."

"Jenna's tired of listening to us bicker on the job site." He frowned at Candice's feet. There could be metal shavings and stray nails on the floor. Not to mention the danger of splinters. "You should put your shoes back on."

"I don't bicker. And I can't put my shoes on."

"Why not? The shoes part." He could debate the bicker part all night long if necessary.

"My feet are swollen. The shoes don't fit anymore."

"Well then sit down." He strode over to the corner of the dining room and pulled one of the padded restaurant chairs from under the tarp. Their red velvet upholstery was faded, and the carved walnut arms would have to be refinished, but they were still very comfortable.

Choosing a relatively clear corner near the windows, he set it down. "Last thing I need is for you to get hurt."

"Always the gentleman."

He retrieved a second chair, then placed one of the tables between the two. "Damn straight."

She picked her way across the room and sat down.

He was both surprised and grateful that she finally did something he asked. He suspected there was a first-aid kit in the kitchen somewhere, but he didn't want to have to look for it because Candy had a nail in her foot.

"Find anything we can use?" she asked.

"Nobody left a screwdriver behind," he replied.

"And, you can't break down the door?"

"You really want me to?"

She sighed, curling her feet beneath her, tucking the dress over her knees. "No. That would be irresponsible. It's a great door."

Derek sat down in the other chair. "My shoulder would probably break before the door anyway. They don't make them like that anymore."

"True." She propped her elbows on the table. "You really think we're that bad?"

"Bad how?"

"Enough of a problem to warrant this." She gestured around the room.

"Tyler's overreacting."

"Maybe it *is* a joke. Maybe he'll be back soon."

Derek doubted that. "Maybe."

Candice brightened. "Good. So, what do we do while we wait?"

"You're asking me? I thought I was a waste of air."

A grin sneaked out on her face. "Did I really say that?"

"More than once."

"Goes to show you how desperate I am."

"You hungry?" He didn't know about Candy, but he hadn't had a chance to eat at the reception. Since they'd exhausted all of the obvious escape plans, and sitting here twiddling their thumbs wasn't going to do any good, they might as well make the best of their captivity.

"What do you mean hungry?" she asked. "Did Tyler leave a picnic I don't know about?"

"We're in a restaurant."

She glanced toward the kitchen, forehead furrowing. "You mean we can…"

"Far as I know, it's still in working order." Derek rose from his chair. Maybe he was wrong. Maybe Tyler would have a change of heart in a couple of hours. In the meantime, there was no need for them to starve.

She peered through the doorway. "You know how to operate that stuff? It looks pretty complicated."

He held a hand out to her. "If you're hungry. I'll cook you something."

"Really?"

"No. I'm a ogre, and I'm toying with you."

"Wouldn't put it past you."

"Come on." He moved closer. "I'll carry you over the danger zone."

"Oh, no you won't."

"Don't get all obstinate on me." Crouching, he slipped one arm around her shoulders and the other under her knees. "Not when I just got you to admit I wasn't a waste of air." He easily hoisted her up, settling her against his chest.

She stiffened. "I never admitted any such thing. Put me down."

"I can put you down. But if you get a nail in your foot, we're going to be in big trouble."

"A nail?"

"It's a construction site."

She glanced suspiciously at the floor. Then her hands went around his neck. "Oh. Well. In that case. Okay."

His footsteps echoed as he paced across the room.

After a moment, Candice relaxed against him, all supple muscles and smooth curves. Her fingers brushed rhythmically against the nape of his neck, and her soft bottom nestled against his stomach. Her skin was warm through the sheer stockings, heating his fingertips.

"Can I make a mighty steed joke?" she asked.

He sucked in a breath and tightened his grip, trying to ignore the glimpse of her creamy cleavage. "Not unless you want to leave yourself wide-open again."

Her clear green eyes widened and an unexpected blush rose in her cheeks as the meaning of his words sank in.

Aha. Her Achilles' heel. If he made it sexy, it kept her quiet.

He'd have to remember that.

NESTLED AGAINST Derek's broad chest, Candice felt as though she'd tumbled into an illicit fantasy. She'd admit to admiring his body on occasion. What woman wouldn't wonder about the feel of his sculpted muscles?

And now she knew.

They were shifting steel. Warm and hard as he easily carried her to the kitchen. Closing her eyes, she gave into temptation and inhaled deeply.

A dark flood of sensuality instantly filled her senses. Derek might be pompous and overbearing, but he was also sexy as sin. Her thighs tingled under his fingers. Her body softened and resistance was replaced by desire.

Too soon, he set her down on the tile floor. As his hand left the small of her back, a taut gaze passed between them, weakening her knees. Her breath stopped for a split second. But then he blinked, and his expression neutralized.

Turning abruptly, he headed for the walk-in freezer, grabbing the lever handle and yanking it forward. The heavy door groaned open, and he flipped the light switch and stepped inside.

Candice followed more slowly, forcing herself to shake off the unsettling feelings. A few seconds of fantasy was one thing, but this was Derek. *Derek.*

He was everything her mother had warned her against—an entrepreneurial shark who only existed to make money and gain power. He ate women like her for lunch.

"Let's scope out our choices," he said from inside the freezer. "Filet mignon, rack of lamb, sockeye salmon, baby back ribs…"

She rubbed her shoulders and curled her toes against the chill of the floor as she gazed at the packed shelves lining the freezer room's walls. "You know how to cook all this stuff?"

"Sure. Don't you?"

Growing up with both a cook and housekeeper on staff had left some definite shortcomings in Candice's homemaking skills. "I'm pretty good with a microwave."

Derek gave her a disapproving frown. "You survive on processed food?"

"Not always." Her teeth chattered for a second. "When I visit my parents, Anna-Leigh sends care packages home with me."

"That's pathetic." He shrugged out of his tux jacket and draped it around her shoulders.

She shook her head, pushing it off. This was getting way too cozy.

His hands held it firm against her shoulder. "Don't be stupid."

"I'm fine."

"Your teeth are chattering."

"We're in a freezer."

He sighed heavily. "Do you *have* to be so stubborn?"

"Do *you* have to be so stubborn?"

"You wear my coat, I'll make you dinner."

"That's—"

"A deal?"

"Fine." She pushed her arms into the sleeves and wrapped the big jacket around her. She had to admit, the body heat lingering in the soft lining felt like heaven. The weight of the fabric pushed comfortingly down on her shoulders.

He flicked open the buttons on his white shirt cuffs and rolled the sleeves over his forearms. Then he moved farther into the hallway-like freezer. "You can't even cook a steak?"

"I don't like steak."

"What do you like?"

"Seafood."

"Hmm." Derek took a few more steps down the shelves.

She stayed put near the open freezer door, soaking up every whiff of warm air that crept in from the kitchen.

He smiled, retrieving a couple of plastic packages. "Lobster ought to do it. You check the refrigerator for butter. I'll light the grill."

"You're going to cook lobster?" Not that she was an expert, but lobster sounded even trickier than steak.

"You bet." He hustled her out of the freezer and closed the door behind them.

She rubbed one cold, stocking-covered foot

against the opposite calf, trying not to feel outclassed. "Didn't you have a cook when you were a kid?"

"Sure we did. Doesn't mean I can't read a recipe book. Go into the fridge and get me some butter, and…" He glanced around the kitchen. It was cluttered with crates and boxes full of new equipment. None had been unpacked yet, since the bulk of the work so far had been in the dining room.

"Never mind," he continued. "I'll find the spices."

By the time Candice got back from the walk-in refrigerator, Derek had the grill flaming and he was stirring a pot on the big stovetop.

"What's that?" She peered around his shoulder, sniffing at the mixture.

"Chocolate."

"You're making chocolate lobster?" Maybe he'd overstated his cooking expertise.

He grinned. "Chocolate mousse for dessert."

"No way." She did cake from a mix sometimes, brownies on an adventurous day.

He slanted her an accusatory look. "Your faith in me is not particularly inspiring."

"But, you always act like such a pampered, spoiled…" Candice bit her lower lip. Here the man was making her a fabulous dinner, and she was insulting him.

"Don't jump to conclusions about people," he said softly.

"Considering how much time we've spent together over the past three months, I didn't think it was *jumping*." Culinary expertise aside, she had ample evidence to back up the fact that he was pampered and spoiled.

He adjusted the flame under the open grill, then flipped a switch to start an exhaust fan above it. "It takes two to tango."

Candice stilled for a split second, overtaken by an image of *tangoing* with Derek, right here, right now, on the dining room floor. She shook it away. The fact that he could cook didn't make him any less dangerous.

"You argued with me over the wood stain," she pointed out.

"You argued right back."

He was right, but she knew you couldn't give an inch with Derek. And it wasn't quite the same thing.

"Honey gloss?" she scoffed. "Natural satin blends with the entire theme, and it's only a halftone off the color you're fighting to the death for."

Derek slowly stirred the pot of melting chocolate. "And honey gloss is only a halftone off the color you're fighting to the death for."

Candice compressed her lips. "It's not the same thing."

"It's exactly the same thing."

He just didn't get it. Natural satin was part of a complex color design. His honey gloss was merely an uninformed, untrained whim.

Or else he was being obstinate. Quite frankly, she suspected the latter. "What about the wainscoting?" What was his excuse for that?

"Your choice is what? A quarter of an inch wider than mine." He unwrapped the lobster tails and set them on the grill. Then he swiftly set out a small pot of butter to melt.

"I'm going for authenticity. Believe me, it makes a difference." She watched his quick, clean movements. "You need some help with that?"

"I'm fine." He crossed the room and retrieved a basting brush from a cutlery drawer. "It makes a whole quarter of an inch difference," he said as he walked back toward her, brandishing the brush for emphasis. "Not to mention several thousand dollars."

"Thanks for not mentioning that."

"No problem." He swirled the brush in the melting butter.

"Why do you care so much?" she asked.

"Why do *you* care so much?" he countered.

"I'm the decorator. It's my job to worry about the details."

"I'm the hotel owner. It's my job to worry about the bottom line."

"I won't go over budget."

"You won't come in under budget, either."

"That's why they call it a budget. I'm going to build you the best restaurant I can within the financial limit you set."

"Nobody's going to notice the damn wainscoting."

"Maybe not specifically—"

"See?" He basted the lobster tails with his left

hand, stirring the chocolate with his right. "Why waste the money on something nobody will notice?"

She dragged her gaze away from his mesmerizing hands. "Not specifically the wainscoting, but they'll notice the overall effect. Like the top of the wine rack. Will some customer walk in and say 'Look, honey, the pattern of the marble on the wine rack flows into the overall scheme of the atrium'? Of course not. But, subconsciously, they'll notice. There's a fine line between four and five stars."

She folded her arms across her chest. "Stick with me, baby, and I'll push you over the top."

Derek stopped stirring and basting, and he stared at her for a moment. The sensual heat in his deep blue eyes was unmistakable. "Left yourself wide-open once again," he whispered low and husky.

She drew back, confused.

A slow smile crossed his face. "Much as I'd like to go 'over the top' with you, *baby*, I don't think it's a good idea, given our current adversarial professional relationship."

Her face heated. "I only meant…"

He chuckled. "I know. But, damn, you give a guy openings that are just too good to pass up."

He turned his attention back to cooking. "Tell you what, in the spirit of cooperation, I'll give on the stain if you give on the wainscoting."

Candice blinked. She didn't plan to give on anything. "But, the wainscoting is—"

"A difference of thousands of dollars." He raised

one eyebrow. "For a quarter of an inch. Can we get a negotiation going here or not?"

Candice was silent for a moment. It wasn't her first choice, but she supposed they could make the wainscoting work. "If you get the wainscoting, I get to choose *all* of the stain and paint colors," she said.

Derek stared at her. "You want me to give you all the stain and paint colors for a mere quarter of an inch?"

"It's thousands of dollars," she countered.

He grinned. "Done." He lifted the spoon out of the chocolate, blowing on the liquid to cool it.

"What do you think?" Cupping his hand several inches below the spoon, he moved it toward her mouth.

She leaned hesitantly forward and licked the tip of the spoon. The rich, dark, sensual chocolate flavor bloomed in her mouth. She closed her eyes and moaned in appreciation.

"Go to the head of the class," she said.

"Why, thank you, teacher." Somehow he made the words sound like a caress.

3

"HAVE YOU CONSIDERED becoming a chef?" Across the candlelit table from Derek, Candice took another bite of her grilled lobster and her lips curved into a blissful smile.

He couldn't help the small surge of pride he felt at her obvious appreciation. "And give up my budding decorating career?"

"No offense," Candice said, lifting her glass of Chablis. "But, you should probably go with your strengths."

"I'm crushed." But he couldn't help grinning.

It was the first time in weeks he'd had time to cook—the first time in months he didn't have to rush off to a meeting or a conference call after dinner. And mental gymnastics with Candice did have their moments. When he was done reaming his brother out for this stunt, he'd have to thank him.

She waved her long-stemmed glass. The lights of downtown Seattle glittered in the distance behind her, and glowing pleasure-boats cruised below on their way back to the marina. "Hey, even you overachievers can't be good at everything."

He sat back in his chair, gazing at her from beneath raised eyebrows. "From a waste of air to an over-achiever all in one night."

"You're still a waste of air when it comes to deco-rating. Accept defeat with dignity and grace."

Derek picked up his own glass of wine, taking a sip. One thing about being locked up in the Light-house Restaurant, they sure didn't need to rough it on the culinary front. "And get the heck away from your renovation job, right?"

She nodded. "Exactly. Why don't you go out and raise some venture capital or something. Leave the restaurant to me."

"Venture capital?"

"I minored in economics."

"You're suggesting I should go out and make money, and you'll stay here and spend it."

"Now you're catching on," she voiced in a singsong, leaning forward. Then she smiled, and her green eyes lit up in the flickering candlelight. Her eyes were bright, her lips were soft and her cheeks were delicately flushed.

For the hundredth time that night he was blown away by her beauty.

"We could have a symbiotic relationship," she said eagerly.

A shot of desire rippled through him. "You're handing me openings on a silver platter again."

"Symbiotic means mutually beneficial." She smirked.

"I know." He could think of *so* many mutually beneficial things he'd like to do to her right now.

His suit jacket had fallen open to reveal her purple dress. The neckline had crept down throughout the course of the evening, and it seemed to cling precariously to the curve of her breasts.

His thoughts kept veering off in inappropriate directions, and he seemed powerless to stop them. He had an almost uncontrollable urge to pull her into his arms. He tightened his grip on the stem of the wineglass.

"The carpet for the crown molding," he said to distract himself. It was a giveaway on his part, but it was the first deal that came to his mind.

"*My* carpet for *your* crown molding?" she asked, sitting up straighter, obviously surprised by the generosity of the deal. Her movement tightened her dress, and he swore he could almost see the pink of one areola.

Derek swallowed a deep draught of wine. "Yeah."

"The vintage, hand-knotted Safavid?"

"Right."

Candice drew a breath, tightening her dress even more. "You won't be sorry."

He was already sorry. Most of his customers wouldn't know a Safavid from a nylon Berber. The best he could hope for was an increase in his carpet-aficionado customer base. Maybe they'd order some extra drinks while dropping down on all fours to run their fingers over the imported fibers.

This round definitely went to her. But only because she was using her breasts as a negotiating tool—even if she didn't realize it.

He had a sudden burning need to make a deal that was weighted on his side of the equation. "Let's talk light fixtures," he said.

"You're not touching my bronze-and-stained-glass chandelier," she warned, eyes narrowing.

"I gave you the carpet."

She shook her head. "That was a completely different deal." Pushing back her chair, she stood up.

Derek jumped up, too. "Where are you going?" He was still worried about her bare feet.

"To get some cocktail napkins."

"Stay here." He motioned with his hand. "I'll get them for you."

He went to the kitchen and retrieved a handful of white paper napkins.

"Got a pen?" she called.

He checked behind the maître d's desk and found a pen.

"What are you planning to do with all this?" he asked as he returned to the table and set the napkins down in front of her.

"Contract amendments." She scooped the pen from his outstretched hand. "The wainscoting for the stain and the crown molding for the carpet."

She printed on a napkin for a moment.

Derek sat down.

"Sign here." She pushed it across the table.

"This is ridiculous."

"Dated and signed by both of us. It ought to hold up in court."

"We're not going to court."

"I'm not taking any chances with my Safavid carpet."

"I'm a man of my word."

She folded her arms across her chest and smiled. "Then you have no reason not to sign, do you?"

Since her crossed arms brought her breasts up against the scooped neck of the dress, and since he could most definitely see soft, pigmented skin peeking out, he did as she asked.

"Perfect." She smiled, scooping up the napkin. "We're finished with those two items." Then she blinked her long lashes. "Any other areas you'd like to discuss?"

He decided then and there to take her along for the next labor negotiation. While he wasn't prepared to say she'd beaten him, he definitely wanted her on the team when the going got tough.

"The light fixtures," he said, deciding it was time for him to win one. He had to concentrate to keep his gaze from dropping to her chest.

"The bronze and stained glass exudes character and history," she began. "When customers enter the Lighthouse, that fixture will be the first thing they see. They'll be overwhelmed by it's grandeur and style. It's a classic. It'll highlight the wine rack—"

"It's a light," he said dryly.

"It's not a *light*." She looked affronted. "Well, yeah, okay, of course it's a light."

"I nearly fell out of my chair when I read the price."

"But, it's not *just* a light. It's an antique."

"Get a reproduction. Nobody will know."

"You'll know."

"I won't care. I'll be too busy spending the money we saved."

Candice leaned forward.

Derek nearly groaned at the cleavage she presented. It ought to be illegal.

Of course, he could tell her, and she'd probably cover up.

Nah.

"I'll know," she said. "I'll care."

"And that's supposed to keep me awake at night?" It wouldn't. Not like the thought of her breasts would.

"Okay. How about this. Restaurant reviewers will know." She leaned back and smiled, obviously appreciating her own brilliance. She lifted her wineglass. "You want them to write about the cheap reproduction or the fine antique."

Derek paused. He needed to succeed in at least one of these side deals, to salvage his pride if nothing else.

"I'll give you the tiles," she said. "The tiles for the light fixture."

"But, I like the tiles."

"Okay." She shrugged. "Suit yourself." She began writing.

"What are you doing?" he asked.

"I'll keep the light fixture. You keep the tiles."

"Wait a minute—"

"Why don't you get the chocolate mousse?" She looked up at him and smiled sweetly. "I wouldn't want to hurt my feet."

"YOU'RE CORRUPT," said Derek as Candice savored the first bite of her chocolate mousse—creamy rich, melting smoothly over her tongue. He should seriously consider a career as a chef.

"Why?" she asked, licking every little morsel off the tip of the spoon.

"You got it both ways on the last deal."

"That's because you were so busy talking to my cleavage." She grasped the top of her dress and tugged it up a little.

His spoon froze in midair. "You knew?"

"*Please.*"

He might be a great cook, but subtlety was not his middle name. The man saw a flash of skin and he was hopeless.

"That's cheating," he said.

"Cheating how?"

"You should have…" He made a lifting motion with both hands.

"*You* could have told me."

A slow, secretive smile grew on his face. "Then you would have covered up."

She smiled back, just as secretively. "Then you

wouldn't have signed away a fifty-thousand-dollar light fixture."

"For fifty thousand dollars, you should have to strut around looking sexy all night."

"Not in the contract." She patted the two signed napkins.

"My mistake."

She chuckled. "It's cleavage, Derek. Every woman at the reception tonight showed off the same thing."

"Not my mother or aunt Eileen."

"Every woman under the age of fifty."

"It's not the same thing."

"Why not?" she asked.

"There's that opening again."

"Are you trying to flirt with me?"

He stared into her eyes for a long, silent moment. "You want me to?"

Danger signs flashed through her mind. No way she was walking into that one. "I want leather upholstery for the dining-room chairs."

"That'll put you over budget."

"How can you know that?"

He tapped his forehead. "Mind like a steel trap. I remember the cost and the square footage required, and the outrageous labor charges."

He did, did he?

She reached up and pulled a couple of pins from her hair, raking her fingertips through the tangled curls. Maybe she could get him to reconsider....

He watched in silence, his gaze following her

every movement. His nostrils flared. "It won't work. But nice try."

"Taking down my hair wasn't a bribe," she lied. "I'm tired, and my head's getting sore. It's after midnight."

His eyebrows crept up. "Uh-huh. Another nice try."

"How long's it been since you had a date?"

"A *what*?"

"A date. You're sure susceptible to a woman who's sitting here doing nothing but minding her own business." She fought a grin.

"I'm not susceptible to anything."

"Uh-huh." She scooped up a small amount of the chocolate mousse with her index finger, then placed it in her mouth, swirling her tongue around the rich cream, then slowly pulling the fingertip back out through her pursed lips. She was shamelessly copying a scene from a movie, but it must have worked because Derek's eyes darkened.

"Stop," he growled.

"Stop what?" She reached for the mousse again.

His hand shot out and he grabbed her wrist. "You're playing with fire."

"I'm eating dessert."

He stared deep into her eyes.

The heat of his hand seared her skin. Her pulse leaped and desire sizzled in her blood.

What was the matter with her? She was locked up alone with him for the foreseeable future, and she was acting like some kind of siren.

"Sorry," she whispered. "I'll stop."

"Good decision." He slowly released her wrist. He sat back and stared out the window, across the black lake to the star-studded sky.

"Derek…"

"Yeah."

"I'm sorry."

He shrugged. "It's okay." He transferred his gaze back to her. "You didn't really do anything."

But, she had.

And, they both knew it.

It was one thing to ignore the fact that her neckline was a little low. It was quite another to make body language promises she had no intention of keeping.

They might be locked up together, and sharing a bottle of wine. But, he was still her client, and her behavior had definitely lacked professionalism.

The sooner this evening ended, the better.

"SLEEP WELL?" asked Candice the next morning, her voice morning-husky.

Derek glanced up from the grill to see her standing in the kitchen doorway. Her purple dress was wrinkled and her hair was in disarray. But she still looked sexy to him.

She stretched her neck and rotated her shoulders, testament to the fact that an old carpet mattress and tablecloth blankets hadn't made the best bed in the world. She'd offered to share it with him, but that was out of the question.

His desire had reached a flash point last night. If she'd so much as brushed a fingertip against him in the night, he'd have kissed her senseless.

At least.

He recognized raw passion when he felt it, and Candice inspired the rawest he'd ever suffered. Taut muscles against the hard floor had made a frustrating night pure hell. But it was better than the alternative.

He flipped a slice of the French bread he was toasting. "Not particularly well. You?"

She shrugged her bare shoulders and padded toward him. "It wasn't too bad. What are you making?"

"Toast." He glanced around the room. His suit coat had to be here somewhere. The sooner he found it, the sooner he could cover her up.

She peeked around his shoulder. "I'm impressed."

He transferred the slices to a waiting plate. Toast and canned orange segments were all he'd found that looked remotely like breakfast.

He forced himself to focus on her hairline. "Want to be even more impressed?"

"Sure."

He turned off the gas grill and headed down the hall. "This way."

"Where are we going?"

"Follow me."

"Why the mystery?"

"All will be revealed in due course," he said, inserting his master key into a small closet.

"You found a way out?"

Oh, great. Now she was going to be disappointed. He sighed. "No. I didn't find a way out."

"Oh."

"But it's something good."

"Yeah?"

He opened the door wide. "Concierge supplies."

"Which are?" She peered into the dark closet.

He flipped the light switch with a flourish. "Toothbrushes, toothpaste, bath products, deodorant, combs." There were also condoms, but he didn't bother listing those. "Anything the weary traveler might have left at home and need from room service."

"Oh…" She scooted in front of him, running her fingers over the cellophane-wrapped packages with obvious reverence. "And we can…" She glanced up at him.

He knew he should step back so he wasn't touching her. But his feet were suddenly frozen to the floor. "Help yourself."

"I think I've died and gone to heaven." She wiggled and shifted as she gathered a handful of toiletries.

Right. She was in heaven, where he was in hell. He had a scantily dressed, bedroom-warm woman pressed up against him, and the last thing in the world he could do was touch her.

He forced a hearty note to his voice. "Men's room is out of commission. So, we'll have to share. You can go first."

She twisted to look at him. "You sure?"

He sucked in a breath. "Absolutely."

IN FRONT OF THE MIRROR in the ladies' room, Candice stripped off her dress, her underwear and her stockings. There was a basket of fluffy white hand towels at one end of the sink, so she doused one in warm water and worked up a lather with some of the floral-scented soap. It wasn't a shower, but it was the next best thing.

She found it hard to believe that Tyler had left them up here all night. Part of her admired his courage. Derek was going to kill him as soon as they got out.

She grinned in the mirror.

Then her smile faltered.

Derek.

Oh, man.

She sure hoped Tyler rescued them soon. Fighting with Derek was bad enough. Developing a case of lust for him was excruciating.

Her skin tingled under the wet towel as she remembered his hot looks. Then she cringed as she remembered her silly, quasi come-on.

What had she been thinking?

She wished she could blame the wine. But, truth was, she'd flat out enjoyed the interest in his eyes. In fact, she'd flat out enjoyed the feeling of playing with fire.

She squeezed the soap out of the towel and rinsed it under warm water, her body tingling as she wiped away the suds. Derek was definitely fire.

The concierge closet had also contained shampoo, so she went to work on her mousse-sticky hair. The process reminded her of summer camp, where upwards of sixty girls had jostled for sink space in the cold-water latrines. Only, the water wasn't cold here. And she had Derek to play with instead of the other girls.

She wondered how he'd take to a game of Truth or Dare.

She quickly pushed the unruly thought from her mind.

Hair and body washed, she slipped back into her dress. She had no choice, unless she wanted to make a sarong out of a tablecloth. But she refused to wear the stockings and underwear.

She filled a sink with water and washed them out. There were a dozen stalls in the restroom, so she headed down to the farthest one and hung the lacy white underwear and sheer stockings up inside. Surely Derek wouldn't venture this far.

Then she tossed her used towels into the basket under the counter and combed out her hair.

CANDICE'S HAIR HAD DRIED to a wavy, golden halo, and her skin looked tanned and healthy in that late afternoon sunlight.

"Okay. This is the big one," she said to Derek, adding yet another recently signed paper napkin to their stack of contract amendments.

"What do you mean the big one?" he asked.

They'd topped a million dollars over an hour ago. He was embarrassed to admit he'd caved on almost everything. But what the hell was a guy supposed to do when the woman across the table wasn't wearing any underwear?

Oh, she'd tried to hide them in the last stall, but he was tall enough to see across the tops of the cubicles. Her stockings and panties were busy drying in the ladies' room. Which meant she was alfresco under that dress, and wreaking havoc on his negotiating skills.

"I want to rip out the wine rack," she said.

"You *what?*" He nearly jumped out of his chair.

"It's in the wrong place, Derek. You—"

"Uh-uh. No way."

"But—"

"Rip it out for the sake of two feet? Are you crazy?" *On top of being nearly naked?*

"It'll ruin the entire—"

"It's *twenty-four inches.*"

"Twenty-four inches is a lot."

"It's this much." He held up his hands.

"But, it ruins the entire flow of the room," she said, turning her palms up in a gesture of frustration.

Derek stared at her in silence. He'd caved on the carpet, the light fixtures, the tablecloths, even the staff uniforms. But this was too much. Tyler had better show up soon.

"I can't do it," he said, shaking his head.

"Tell me what you want," she quickly countered.

He sure as hell wasn't about to do that.

"There must be something," she pressed.

He stared into her crystal-green eyes.

There was one thing. A favor he'd thought of in the middle of the night. Not the one where she was naked on a tropical island for a couple of months. Though he'd arrange that in an instant if he thought she'd go for it.

This was a personal favor. It didn't have anything to do with the restaurant contract.

"What?" she prompted.

"You really want to know?" he asked slowly, considering whether or not he should even broach the subject.

She nodded.

He sat up straight, squaring his shoulders. "Here's my deal." He carefully lifted the stack of signed napkins containing the details of nearly twenty-four hours worth of negotiations. Then he looked deep into her eyes. "We rip these up."

"No way." She grabbed for them, but he pulled them out of her reach.

"In exchange," he said. "I give you carte blanche."

"What do you mean?"

"You get everything you want."

"You mean within budget."

He shook his head. "No budget—"

"But—"

"—limit."

"*What?*"

"No budget limit. You do anything you want, and you have unlimited funds to do it with."

"But… How…" She suddenly compressed her lips and eyed him with suspicion.

"It's not sex," he said dryly.

"I never thought—"

"Sure you did."

She smiled self-consciously. "Okay. But, only for a second."

He grinned in return. "I want you to take me home for a visit with your father."

She stared at him in silence. "Why?"

"The Enoki electronics deal."

"I can't force my family to make a deal with you."

"I'm not asking you to."

"I only own five percent of the company, Derek. And I've been a silent partner all my life."

"All I want is a chance to talk to your father. Outside of the office, in a casual setting. You just have to pretend we're friends."

"Friends?"

"I know it's a stretch."

"It's not that," she said.

"Then, what is it?"

"I would never, *ever* compromise my family for personal gain."

"You're not compromising anybody. It's a good deal for them, too."

Her expression turned suspicious. "Then why do you need my help?"

"Because I know they won't hear me out. Not after I blocked his rezoning application last year."

"That was you?"

Derek felt a flicker of hope. "He doesn't know it was me?"

"I'm sure *he* knows it was you. But I never pay attention to that stuff."

Derek's momentary optimism died. "Right. So you can see what I'm up against."

She sat back in her chair. "How does that saying go? You've made your bed…"

"All I'm asking you to do is help me fluff the pillows."

"I'm your decorator, not your housekeeper."

"This will be good for both of us. Way it works is, Hammond Electronics won the contract to supply Enoki Communications with hardware for their three hundred Far-East outlets."

"Telling me about the deal isn't going to help."

Derek frowned. That made no sense. Understanding the deal was everything. "I'm explaining how it'll be good for your family."

She shook her head. "Doesn't matter."

"How can it not matter? What I want to propose is a partnership. Reeves-DuCarter International owns a spectrum license in Asia. If Hammond Electronics and Reeves-DuCarter can agree on a set of specifications instead of supplying a generic, we can set up a network and become a real player in the wireless market, long-term. If they interface with our equipment, they'll end up with a proprietary market share."

Her eyes started to glaze over.

"Candy?"

"I'm *not* helping you swing a deal with my father."

"I'm not asking you to help me swing a deal. I'm asking for an introduction." Derek paused. "An introduction, a dinner and you get a dream renovation."

"By selling out my family."

Derek threw up his hands. "You're *not* selling out *anybody*. Haven't you been listening to a word I said? All I want is the introduction. I'll take it from there. If they say no, they say no."

Candice straightened, and a calculating smile grew on her face. "Okay. I'll make you a deal."

Oh, great. Why did he get the feeling he was going to get duped again?

Don't think about her missing underwear.

Her hand went to her stomach. "I'm starving. You throw in another dinner, and I'll introduce you to my father." She started to write something down on a new napkin.

Dinner?

All she wanted was dinner?

He could do dinner. He'd do a hundred dinners.

But, wait a minute. That was too easy. He eyed up her complacent expression. She got dinner thrown into the bargain? Well, he wanted a little quid pro quo….

"Okay," he countered, covering her hand to stop her from writing. "I'll throw in dinner, and several million dollars, if you'll seal the deal with a kiss instead of a napkin."

"You won't give it to me in writing?"

"I'm a man of my word."

She stared at his lips for a minute, blinking uncertainly.

"I'll make it easy," he said, worried about her hesitation, not wanting to blow everything on a technicality. "I'll make the dinner. You rank it on a scale of zero to ten. I get one kiss for every point."

Her eyes went round. "Deal."

She couldn't get the word out fast enough. And her incredulous expression told Derek he'd just lost the kiss.

But he'd gained the introduction. And, he would have made dinner anyway.

4

IT WAS REALLY TOO BAD she had to give it a zero, because this was one of the best meals of Candice's life.

Derek had spent a good half hour setting out a fresh tablecloth, china, silverware and candles. He'd dimmed the lights, and the sky had cooperated by giving them a gorgeous sunset followed by a rising full moon.

He'd barred Candice from the kitchen while he cooked.

Then, he'd produced crab-stuffed mushrooms, grilled salmon in béarnaise sauce, saffron rice and asparagus. And he'd obviously raided the high end of the wine cellar. She was going to remind the chef tomorrow morning to keep plenty of Andollin chardonnay on hand. It was magnificent.

"I can't believe Tyler's left us here this long." At this rate, she'd be able to talk to the chef before she went home for a shower.

"I can," said Derek.

"Is he that vindictive?"

"Stubborn, not vindictive. Besides, he probably forgot about us a long time ago."

"Oh, those newlyweds." Candice shook her head in mock disapproval.

"And, he did accomplish his objective."

"How so?"

Derek lifted his wineglass in a toast. "We're not going to fight on the job site anymore and upset Jenna."

"That's because you won't *be* on the job site anymore."

"I may drop in from time to time."

"But, not to give advice." She wanted to be clear on that.

He made a zipping motion across his mouth.

Candice's gaze caught and held on his firm lips. It was really too bad she had to give dinner a zero. They looked incredibly kissable.

She took a final bite of the salmon and the smooth-textured sauce.

All things considered, a zero was a pretty harsh score. After all, he'd gone to a whole lot of trouble. And, this would—her gaze found his lips again—in all likelihood, be her one and only chance.

Okay, so she had kissed him once before. If you could count that fleeting peck in the Tunnel of Love. She didn't know who had been more surprised then. Her at the unexpected arc of attraction, or him at what was obviously a sudden recognition of the Hammond name.

Having somehow figured out he was about to make out with the daughter of his archenemy, he'd bounced back faster than a burn reflex. No real kissing had been accomplished. But it had *sure* been interesting.

Maybe now was the time to finish the job.

Maybe she should give him a one.

She took another sip of the crisp white wine while she thought about it. "We probably won't see much of each other after tonight," she ventured.

"You still have to introduce me to your family," he reminded her.

"Right. Of course." She was guaranteed to see him at least one more time. Though, she could hardly kiss him in front of her parents.

So there it was.

She should go for a one.

She took a bite of the saffron rice, noting that the spicing was absolutely perfect. Maybe a two. One point for the salmon and one for the rice.

Of course, the wine deserved something, too. This was a tough call.

"I won't let you back out on the introduction," he said.

"I'm an honorable woman."

"That's good to know."

Even if she was going to grossly underscore his meal.

She took a bite of the asparagus. It was tender, slightly crisp, and perfectly complemented by the sauce. She really had to give it a point.

That was three. Or was it four?

Four kisses.

She let her vision blur on the candle flame. Four kisses was the very least she owed him. What could it hurt? It wasn't like she was kissing him out of passion or desire. It was only a business deal.

Besides, they'd be out of here tomorrow morning. And, after that, there was one chaste dinner at her parents' house, and he'd be pretty much out of her life.

The thought depressed her slightly.

Which was silly. All they ever did was argue.

"Ready for dessert?" he asked.

Candice blinked out of her contemplation. "Sure. What did you make?"

"Crème brûlée." He stood up to head for the kitchen.

Uh-oh. She had the feeling that another kiss was coming up.

That made five. She took a bracing sip of wine while she watched him walk away.

Five kisses. Fifty percent. Somehow, fifty percent seemed churlish. He'd worked awfully hard.

Derek returned from the kitchen, a small bowl of crème brûlée in each hand. He bent at the waist and set the dessert down in front of her, arranging the bowl just so. He gave her a knowing grin, holding her gaze. He was all but daring her to give him a zero for the dessert.

She pulled back before she did something stupid like tell him his score and dive right in. "Thank you," she said instead, gesturing to the bowl.

"Hope you enjoy it." There was a twinkle in his eyes.

"I'm sure—" She pressed her lips together. He'd nearly backed her into a corner, admitting the dessert was good before she'd even tasted it. "Nice try."

Derek's grin widened. "It's my mother's favorite recipe."

"That's nice."

"If you don't like it, she'll be crushed."

"Foul." She couldn't help but return his grin. One point. That was all the dessert was getting. She didn't care whose mother would be disappointed.

"There are seconds if you want them." He finally drew back a little.

"I'm sure this'll be fine."

"Oh. It'll be more than fine." He slipped back into his own chair and picked up a silver spoon.

Candice dipped hers into the smooth cream. She lifted a small bite to her mouth. She tested it with the tip of her tongue and was catapulted to another level of flavor.

"Holy…" She raised her fingers to her lips.

"What did I tell you?"

Candice stared down at the simple dessert. "How did she…"

"Family secret," said Derek. "Enjoy."

Candice took another bite. There was no way in the world she could give the crème brûlée less than full marks. Which made six kisses. A trill of excitement tightened her chest. Good thing she'd had enough wine to see her through this.

"She used to make it on Christmas Day," Derek continued. "The neighbors would come from miles around to join us for dessert."

"I don't blame them," said Candice, finishing every last morsel.

"Seconds?" asked Derek.

"Wish I could." She shook her head.

He leaned back in his chair, taking up his wine-glass. "So?"

"What?" She faked confusion.

"How many points are we talking?"

"You took a big chance on this."

"I had a secret weapon."

"The crème brûlée?"

He shook his head. "Your honor."

"I could give you a zero."

"You could."

But she wouldn't. Now that she'd made up her mind, she intended to do it right. Besides, the expression on his face was going to be worth it. She loved shooting him curveballs.

"Zero to ten," Derek said softly, taking a slow sip of the chardonnay.

Candice squared her shoulders. "Ten."

Ten?

Derek nearly choked on the wine, inhaling half liquid, half air. He'd hoped for a one, maybe a two. He couldn't have heard her properly.

"Ten?" he parroted.

Her eyebrows rose. "What? Am I calling your bluff?"

Not hardly. He just couldn't believe she was serious. "Deal's a deal, Derek."

This had to be a joke. He silently scrutinized her expression. There had to be a catch. "I don't get it."

She reached for the pen and a fresh napkin, and scrawled the number ten, large and bold, holding it up in front of the candle. "Does it help to have it in writing?"

Yeah. It did.

Derek slowly rose from his chair, still on guard for the punch line. "Ten kisses?"

She looked him straight in the eyes. "Right."

He pointed back and forth. "You and me."

There was a challenge in her nod. "Uh-huh."

"What's the catch?"

She rose to face him, pushing the armchair out of the way. "No catch."

"But we fight."

"I guess we're making up."

He stopped mere inches away, close enough that he could smell her wildflower shampoo, feel the heat from her body, appreciate the texture of her smooth skin. She was stunningly gorgeous, sexy as hell and he was suddenly afraid that fighting with her might have been a defense mechanism.

"This is going to change things between us," he warned.

Her green eyes danced. "Maybe. Depends on the kisses."

His eyebrows shot up. "That a dare, Candy?"

"It's a fact, Derek."

"Talk about pressure."

"I hear you work well under pressure."

She did, did she?

Filling his lungs, Derek slid his palm across her cheek, cupping her face as he took a step forward, snaking the other arm around her slim waist. "As a matter of fact, I work great under pressure."

He dipped toward her mouth, puckered and touched his lips to hers. The first kiss was gentle. At least, it started out gentle. And he managed to keep it that way for all of five seconds.

But then her lips unexpectedly parted, and he tasted the sweetness of her mouth—a shot of ambrosia that ignited his blood and sent a sharp flash of desire coursing the length of his legs.

He pulled her flush against his hips and tunneled his fingers back into her hair. It was soft and fragrant. Her curves were supple, and the essence of her bombarded his senses.

He went straight to kiss number two, or maybe they were still on one. Did it count when he took a breath? Their lips hadn't exactly parted.

He slipped his hand beneath the jacket—a warm cocoon of silky dress and tuxedo lining. He wished he could crawl in after it. As his hand brushed the curve of her buttocks, he remembered the missing panties. His arousal jacked up another degree.

When her hands tentatively touched his shoulders, the city lights blended into a laser show behind his eyes. His body hardened. The hand at the small of her back convulsed, pressing her soft stomach against the hardness of his arousal.

She didn't resist. She melted. Her lips parted farther, and he slipped his tongue inside. A murmur sounded in her throat, fueling his passion as her tongue responded to his coaxing.

The oxygen left his body. The room dimmed, and he felt the outer sections of his brain shut down. Nothing existed except the taste, the scent, the softness of Candy. He kept on kissing, wider, harder, arching her back.

The hands on his shoulders tightened, each fingertip sending individual shock waves into his body. All those weeks, all those months of verbal sparring, testing the limits, intellectual foreplay. He had no idea how he'd made it this long without kissing her properly.

The candlelight wavered. The scent of the melting wax blended with her perfume. The sound of his own heartbeat roared in his ears. And he couldn't get enough of her taste. He opened wider, delved deeper, pulled her more tightly against him.

Her fingertips inched across the nape of his neck. She tipped her head to one side, moaning his name against his mouth.

And he wrapped his arms fully around her, lifting her from the floor. Her dress slipped up, and his fingertips contacted heat from her bare thighs. Sensation slammed through his body with the force of a tidal wave. The point of no return shimmered on the horizon.

Through sheer force of will, he broke the kiss, setting her gently to her feet as he drew back. Her jewel-bright eyes were glazed, her pupils slightly dilated. Their deep breathing synchronized as they stared at each other in disbelief.

Her tongue flicked out to test her swollen lips.

"One," she whispered.

Derek's hands slid up and closed convulsively around her rib cage, his thumbs just beneath her breasts. He couldn't decide whether to hold her away or pull her back. His voice was a hoarse whisper that seemed stuck in his chest. "We've got trouble."

She wrapped her fingers around his biceps, coming up on her toes, her voice smooth and as rich as the crème brûlée. "Derek, we've had trouble from the second we met."

He had to agree with her there.

He took a deep breath, made a totally self-indulgent decision, and leaned in for another kiss. This one was harder and hungrier than the first. His thumbs teased the undersides of her breasts, itching to make their way up to her coral nipples.

Kissing, he reminded himself. The deal was for kissing *only*.

Even if it was damn near orgasmic kissing.

She tasted of sweet cream and smelled like wild-flowers. Her lips were soft and moist and welcoming, and her lithe body fit to the cradle of his thighs.

He moved his lips to her neck, making his way along her smooth shoulder, tasting her skin, testing, inhaling until he made it to the bare tip.

The dress slipped an inch, and the top of her creamy white breasts were exposed to his view. He straightened, staring for a moment. Then he closed his eyes against the torture, resting his forehead against hers, drawing in deep, desperate breaths.

She shifted, and he felt her lips on his neck, soft, butterfly-light touches that had the power to scorch his soul. Her tongue brushed his sensitive skin, and his thumbs crept inexorably up the undersides of her breasts.

She wrapped her arms around his neck, burrowing her face in the crook. Her sweet, hot breath fanned his skin, and he gritted his teeth to keep from tearing off her clothes.

He cupped one breast, and she moaned his name. If she'd come anywhere near that sound the first day they had met, he'd have been her slave for the past three months. He slipped his hand inside the neckline of her dress, thrumming his fingertips over her nipple. It tightened in response, and he groaned in true pain.

He kissed her mouth again, trying to appease the raging storm within him. His hunger was raw, his need intense. The desire to push her back on the makeshift bed and bury himself was almost overpowering.

In another second, he'd…

He sucked in a breath and forced himself to pull back, breaking the kiss. "We *have* to stop," he rasped.

Her emerald eyes blinked up at him in confusion, her face soft and vulnerable in the flickering candlelight. "What was that? Did we hit ten?"

"That was me hitting break point."

He let her go and raked his hand through his hair. "Either we back off *right* now and take up neutral corners, or I grab a handful of condoms and we go for it."

He held his breath, hoping against hope she'd go for the condoms. It would be crazy, stupid, irresponsible, but he wanted her more than anything in his life.

She slowly nodded, taking a step back.

She swallowed. "Right."

Right *what?* he nearly screamed.

Her hand went to her forehead. "I don't know what I was thinking."

He was pretty sure that meant no condoms, but he waited on tenterhooks for another second.

She shook her head. "We have to forget all about this."

Crushing disappointment shot through Derek, before he sucked it up. "Of course."

She moved to the table and blew out the candle.

Derek stayed frozen, afraid his tense muscles would shatter if he tried to move.

She slipped the strap back up on her shoulder. "We'll go to sleep. We'll get out of here tomorrow morning. And everything can go back to normal."

"And our deal?"

She turned to gaze at him in silence, and he longed to close his eyes against the temptation she presented.

"Carte blanche for an introduction to your family?" he elaborated.

"Deal's a deal," she whispered.

5

CANDICE DESPERATELY NEEDED a way out of the damn deal.

She pedaled her bike for all she was worth, stretching out the distance between her and Jenna as they headed up Briar Hill on a cool, sunny Saturday morning.

It had been two weeks since the construction crew liberated them from the Quayside, and she hadn't seen Derek since. With him out of the picture, things were moving smoothly on the renovation.

Too bad the same couldn't be said for her life.

Derek's kisses had left her tense, humming with nervous energy. She couldn't seem to sit still during the day. And when she closed her eyes at night, his image danced in front of her eyes. Instead of sleeping, she saw his face, heard his voice, felt his touch.

It was everything she'd ever feared, and worse. When she was twenty, she'd watched in shock and disbelief as her best friends fell for cold-hearted business sharks. She'd begged them to walk away, but they'd flittered around the wealthy objects of their in fatuation until their hearts had been trampled into the dust.

Candice had sworn it would never happen to her. And she wasn't about to let it.

Her thigh muscles burned as she approached the crest of the hill. But she kept on pumping, kept on pushing. Maybe if she pushed hard enough, she'd sleep tonight. At some point, sheer physical exhaustion would counteract the mental torture. Wouldn't it?

Too soon, the road ended at the Briar Park parking lot. Leaving the traffic behind, she slowed to a stop, dismounting onto shaking legs before pushing her front wheel into the iron bike rack. She drew deep, rapid breaths, walking in small circles on the grass while she waited for her heart rate to get back to normal.

She should have regretted their close call. Instead, the memory turned her on. So much so that she knew she had to stay away from him or risk becoming a moth to his flame.

Which meant she couldn't set up the meeting with her family. Which meant she wasn't living up to her end of the bargain. Which meant sooner or later, Derek was going to figure that out and get angry.

She pushed her sweaty hair back from her forehead. She'd already blown off several of his phone calls, one three days ago and another yesterday morning. Call her crazy, but she suspected he was about to run out of patience.

Jenna pulled up to the bike rack. "You training for the triathlon, or what?" she gasped.

"Ate too many cookies last night," Candice lied. She hadn't shared the details of the restaurant kisses with Jenna or anyone else.

Jenna parked her bike. "I think you just wore off an entire dozen."

"I wish." Candice stretched from side to side, the ocean breeze cool against her bare limbs.

Jenna stretched, too. Then she nodded at the Java Hut, a popular coffee shop that sat in the middle of the small park. "You up for oatmeal-raisin?"

Comfort food sounded good to Candice. "Sure."

They locked their bikes and headed down the gravel pathway.

Risky or not, Candice knew that avoiding Derek was her only hope. She couldn't imagine sitting through an evening with him at her parents' house. And Lord help her if he actually managed to cut a deal with her father. She'd never get a decent night's sleep again.

Jenna pointed toward the octagonal coffee shop. "Oh, good, there's Tyler."

Candice's gaze darted down the pathway. Her heart slid to her toes and her mouth went dry. Derek.

"You told *Tyler* we were coming here?" she squeaked at Jenna.

"Of course."

And Tyler had told Derek. Two degrees of separation. Derek could find her any old time he wanted. And it looked like he wanted.

Jenna glanced at Candice's expression, then did a double take. "What's wrong?"

Candice didn't answer. Derek was here. In a few seconds, she was going to have to face him, talk to him, lie to him….

"You look like you saw a ghost," said Jenna.

"It's nothing," said Candice.

"You and Derek fighting again?"

"How could we fight? He hasn't been on the job site for two weeks."

Jenna tightened her ponytail. "You seen him outside of work?"

"No."

"Then what is it?"

Candice focused on the pathway directly in front of her. The wind picked up off the ocean, and a few cars zoomed by on the side streets as their footsteps crunched on the gravel. "Nothing."

"Here they come," Jenna whispered in her ear. "Give, or I'll ask Derek."

Candice slid a glare in Jenna's direction. "Fine. I promised I'd take him to my parents' house. Something about an electronics deal."

Jenna looked disappointed. "That's it?"

"I haven't gotten around to it yet, and I know he's going to be upset."

"He's not an ogre, you know."

Candice compressed her lips. Yeah. She knew that now. Which only made things worse. "I don't think our relationship is ever going to be easy."

Jenna patted her on the shoulder. "Well, work on it, will you? You're my best friend and he's my brother-in-law. I want you to find some common ground."

If you asked Candice, they had a little *too* much common ground at the moment.

"I'd hate to have to lock you up again," said Jenna.

"Like that's ever going to happen," Candice scoffed, though she shrank a little inside at the thought.

"Okay, I'll admit, Tyler got a little carried away."

"A *little?*"

"It worked," said Jenna.

"Not exactly."

"Things are a whole lot better now."

Candice supposed that depended on your definition of *better*. A shape suddenly loomed in her peripheral vision, and she stopped short before running squarely into Derek's broad chest.

Tyler reached for Jenna's hand, drawing her up against him. "Hey, sweetheart."

Candice could feel Derek's intense stare.

When he spoke, his tone was strikingly formal for someone who had nearly found her tonsils. "Hello, Candice."

She scrunched her eyes shut, putting it off for a heartbeat, but then she had no choice but to turn and face the inevitable.

He was angry all right. His blue eyes were crystal-hard, his lips pursed tight, and a small muscle ticked in the top of his right cheek. Apparently, people didn't often ignore his phone calls.

"Hi," she returned on a forced breezy note, tipping her chin, refusing to acknowledge his mood.

Beside them, Tyler wrapped Jenna into a tight hug. The two laughed and whispered in their embrace, like they'd been apart for weeks instead of hours.

Candice caught Derek's eye, and their gazes locked. An instant avalanche of emotion swept through her and she was catapulted back two weeks. For a bizarre second, she imagined herself walking into his arms.

"You didn't call me back," he said.

She shook off the unruly feelings and squared her shoulders. "I tried."

Derek's mouth curved into a cold half smile. He gave his head an almost imperceptible shake, and his eyes called her a liar.

He probably had a receptionist, a secretary and voice mail. Like she wouldn't have been able to leave a dozen messages if she'd tried.

"Can we talk inside?" asked Jenna, pulling back from Tyler. "I'm starting to get a chill."

The wind had freshened and Candice's damp T-shirt clung coldly to her stomach, reminding her she was sweaty and smelly. She was also lying through her teeth. She hated it when Derek had the upper hand.

Jenna and Tyler started ahead.

"Arranged the meeting yet?" asked Derek, turning to walk toward the Java Hut.

"Not yet," said Candice, falling into step.

"What's the holdup?"

"Haven't had time."

"We had a deal."

She rubbed her rapidly chilling arms, keeping her focus face-forward. "You didn't say anything about timing."

Derek snorted. "Yeah right. Like I can afford to sit around and wait—"

"That's it, isn't it?" Candice jumped on the opening, trying for the offensive instead of the defensive.

He drew back, squinting in confusion. "What's it?"

"It's all about *afford* for you."

"What are you talking about?"

She gave her head a pitying shake. "I know your type. You're obsessive, fixated on money. You have to break everything down into dollars and cents."

He came to a halt on the coffee shop porch, where the building blocked the wind and the September sun instantly felt warmer. Instead of taking up the argument, he reached into his shirt pocket and pulled out his cell phone.

"Call them, Candy."

She glanced up in disbelief. "Now?"

"Now."

"But…"

Tyler and Jenna had disappeared through the heavy front door.

Derek cocked his head and stared down at Candice—immovable, implacable and in the right.

Resigned, Candice snatched the phone from his hand. "Fine."

She flipped it open and dialed her parents' house,

glaring at Derek the whole time. She hated his confident posture, his cocksure expression, the way he simply *expected* the world to do his bidding.

It wasn't fair that the world fell at his feet. It also wasn't fair that he could act like a jerk and give her butterflies at the same time.

"Hammond residence."

"Anna-Leigh? It's Candice. Is Mom around?"

"She sure is. Let me get her for you."

Candice turned away, but it didn't help. She could still feel Derek's stare penetrating her skin. She felt like an over-revved engine about to blow.

"Candice?"

"Hey Mom."

"How are you, dear?"

She forced herself to calm down and focus on her mother. "I'm great. How about you guys?"

"Not too bad."

Candice nodded. "Good. Good."

"Your dad just got back from Texas."

"Really?"

"He bought a bull."

Now that seriously distracted Candice's attention. "A *what*?"

"Captain Fantastic."

She could hear the resignation in her mother's tone. Her dad prided himself on quickly spotting and acting on good business opportunities. It had led to some interesting periods in their lives. But buying a bull was strange, even for him.

"Why'd he do that?" she asked.

"Apparently the owner was willing to deal, and the semen is very valuable."

"Semen?" asked Candice.

Derek shifted around to stare at her, forehead furrowing.

"It's a breeding bull," her mother explained.

"Right… And you're going to keep it…"

"This is where it gets interesting," said her mother.

"I can't wait," said Candice.

Derek made a hand motion, telling her to move it along.

She ignored him.

"He wants to buy the ranch," said her mother.

"In *Texas?*"

"Saves moving Captain Fantastic."

"Well, as long as he's thought it all through."

Her mother laughed. "I told him there'd better be air-conditioning if he expected me to visit."

"What did he say?" asked Candice.

Derek rolled his eyes and threw up his hands.

"He's installing air-conditioning."

"Oh, Mom." Candice tried not to laugh.

"Not to worry. Couple of weeks. A month, tops. Then he'll have worked out his bull lust, and we'll get back to normal. On the bright side, I'm sure the ranch staff will appreciate the air-conditioning long-term. Now, what can I do for you, honey?"

Candice shook her head. She loved her father dearly, and she had no doubt the bull venture would make money. But there were times when she didn't know how her mother put up with his impulsive schemes. "I was wondering if you and Dad are free next—"

"Tonight," said Derek.

Candice blinked at him.

"Tonight," he repeated.

She gritted her teeth. "Tonight," she said into the phone.

"You thinking of dropping by?" asked her mother.

"Yeah. I have this—"

"Oh, do. Come for dinner. Your father's dying to tell somebody *all* about Captain Fantastic."

Discuss bull semen over dinner?

Candice felt her body relax for the first time in two weeks. A slow grin grew on her face. It would serve Derek darn well right. "I was thinking of bringing along a friend."

"Does your friend know anything about cattle breeding?"

"I'll ask."

"See you tonight, then."

"Bye, Mom." Candice clicked off the phone and handed it back to Derek.

"We're on?" Derek asked.

"We're on," she announced as she headed for the coffee shop door. This was perfect. If her dad was bull-obsessed this week, he wasn't going to be the least bit interested in making a wireless communications deal with Derek.

As soon as the renovation was done, Derek *would* be out of her life.

"What's so funny?" Derek asked, falling into step behind her, grabbing the top of the door panel as she pulled on the handle. The weight instantly disappeared from her hand.

"Nothing," she said and walked into the brightly lit coffee shop.

Plants decorated every nook and cranny of the octagonal room. The furniture was light, the colors crisp, and big windows overlooked the ocean.

"What was that conversation all about?" asked Derek as they started toward Jenna and Tyler's table.

"Girl talk."

"Semen?"

Candice nodded. "Sure. Mom and I talk semen all the time."

Derek choked out a disbelieving laugh.

"What do you and your dad talk about?" she asked.

"The NASDAQ index."

"You need a life, Derek."

"I have a life, Candy."

DEREK HAD a perfectly fine life.

Contrary to what Candice and Tyler might think, he didn't need a steady girlfriend, and he didn't need to discuss reproduction with his parents.

What he needed was to keep *all* the divisions of Reeves-DuCarter firmly in the black. And right now that meant nailing down a wireless agreement with Chuck Hammond.

It also meant keeping his focus. Which meant keeping his craving for Candy under control. Which was going to be a whole lot easier to do once tonight was over.

He watched from his car as she walked out the front door of her apartment building. Her low-cut khaki jeans clung to the curve of her hips. They were topped with a short olive-green jacket—its double zipper revealing the curve of her breasts at one end and a wink of her navel at the other. It was obvious she wore nothing beneath.

Gritting his teeth, he opened the driver's side door and rounded the hood to meet her. Was she doing this on purpose?

"Casual?" he drawled, refusing to acknowledge how sexy she looked in the simple outfit. The only jewelry she wore was a teardrop silver necklace and two pairs of stud earrings made of emerald-colored glass. Her blond hair was just tousled enough to scream sensuality.

She reached for the door handle of his black Porsche, but he beat her to it.

"It's a nice night," she said sliding into the passenger seat. "They'll probably barbecue."

Derek glanced down at his white shirt and charcoal jacket. "You could have said something."

She grinned, unrepentantly. "Are you kidding?"

As he rounded the car again, Derek tugged at his

tie. He stripped off his suit jacket and laid it behind the front seat. Then he unbuttoned his collar and rolled up his sleeves.

He folded his body into the driver's seat and pulled the door shut. "That do?"

Candice cocked her head and tucked her hair behind one ear. "You've still got that intense, shark look about you. But I don't suppose you can help it."

He pushed in the clutch and turned the ignition key. "Some would call that alert intelligence."

"Some would call it predation."

Derek pulled out onto the street. "It's a jungle out there, baby."

Candy laughed, and the sound hit him right in the solar plexus. He'd just discovered a serious weakness for laid-back sexy. His fingers were itching to pull down the thick silver zipper and slip inside to touch her smooth, tanned skin. He wanted to trace her pouty lips with the pad of his thumb, then taste them until he'd had his fill.

"Left on Blanchard," she said.

He switched lanes. Too bad seducing Candy was at cross-purposes to making a deal with her father. For that matter, seducing Candy was at cross-purposes to staying sane.

As usual, he had facts and figures, projections and rationale neatly stored in his brain for tonight's discussion. He needed to focus on business, not on the texture of Candy's skin.

It only took ten minutes to get to her parents'

house, but it was ten very long minutes. They lived in a big old brownstone, set back from the road, behind a cedar hedge in an old-money neighborhood.

He turned into the curved driveway. "This where you grew up?"

She grimaced. "This is it."

Derek raised his eyebrows. "Poor little rich girl?"

"Come on, Derek. You know money's not all it's cracked up to be."

"Are you kidding? Money's everything it's cracked up to be. Money gives you freedom, flexibility, options."

"Are you telling me you'd be miserable without money?"

"No. But if I didn't have money, I'd sure spend a lot of time trying to make some."

"You have money, and you still spend all your time trying to make it."

Derek grinned as he pulled to a stop in the turnaround in front of the house. "That's so I can have more."

"What are you going to do with more?"

"Haven't decided yet."

They opened their doors simultaneously, and Derek caught up with her on the wide concrete staircase.

"Don't you think you're a little greedy?" she asked.

"Not in the least. I'd be greedy if I hoarded my money and only used it on myself. I don't do that. I open companies, create jobs...hire decorators."

"Low blow."

"Having money isn't a sin. Neither is knowing how to make it—particularly if you use it responsibly." He shrugged. "Somebody's got to put the right resources in the right places to keep the economic engines of this country running."

She glanced back at the Porsche. "For a philanthropist, you have very expensive toys."

He grinned. Hell, he wasn't perfect. He liked expensive wine, too. "Guilty as charged."

She reached for the handle of the arched double doors.

"Any last minute advice about your father?" he asked.

"He's a lot like you."

Derek relaxed a little. "Intelligent man?"

She tipped her head back to look at him. "Intense. Hungry. Big ego."

A jolt of desire coursed through Derek's system. Intense and hungry was exactly how he felt. Her lips were only inches away. The soft curve of her throat was exposed, and from this angle, he couldn't see even the slightest tan line on her breasts. Did she sunbathe in the nude? Did she have *any* clue about her effect on men?

Luckily, before he could do anything stupid, she pushed the door open. "Hey, Mom. We're here," she called in a loud voice.

"On the deck," answered a woman's voice from the depths of the house.

Candy dumped her small tote bag on a table in the entry hall. "Follow me."

The house was large, and the architecture grandiose, but the soft furnishings, fresh flowers and whimsical knickknacks made it feel homey and inviting. Derek followed Candy past a large, arched-ceiling living room, down a wide hallway to a white covered veranda. Overlooking an expanse of lush lawn, it was dotted with potted palms and furnished with deep-cushioned rattan couches and wooden folding tables.

Candy's mother was arranging flowers on a dining table, while her father adjusted dials on a stainless-steel gas barbecue.

"Mom, Dad, I'd like you to meet my friend Derek Reeves. Derek, these are my parents. Nancy and Chuck Hammond."

Nancy was dressed in a pair of white pants, with a nautical-look blue-and-white striped shirt. Chuck was wearing brand-new blue jeans and a pearl-snapped plaid shirt that could have come straight out of a rodeo parade.

Nancy quickly looked up from the flowers and smiled at Derek, then her questioning glance shifted to Candy.

Uh-oh. Derek hadn't considered how this might look.

Chuck strode forward. "I take it you're more commonly known as Derek Reeves-DuCarter?" He held out his hand.

Derek shook the man's hand with a firm grip. "Sometimes."

Chuck's attention shifted back and forth between Derek and Candy. "Well, well, well. Isn't this cozy— in a Shakespearean sort of way."

Derek let go of Chuck's hand and spoke heartily. "Nothing at all like that."

"Nothing like what?" asked Candy.

"We're acquaintances," said Derek. "Cand…ice is redecorating a restaurant for Reeves-DuCarter."

"The Quayside," Candy put in.

"Of course," said Nancy, reaching out to offer her own hand to Derek. "She's mentioned it to us. We're delighted to meet you. Chuck, can we pour some drinks?"

Chuck smiled fondly at his daughter. "I've got a pitcher of special martinis."

"Yum," she answered.

Chuck raised his eyebrows at Derek.

"A martini is fine with me."

"I'll get the chilled glasses," said Nancy as the pair headed through a set of French doors.

Candy leaned toward Derek. "Shakespearean?"

"Romeo and Juliet."

"What?"

"The Montagues and the Capulets."

She blinked at him in confusion.

"The Hammonds and the Reeves-DuCarters. They think we're a couple."

"Why would they think that?"

"How many men have you brought home to meet them lately?"

Candy's lips pursed. "Oh."

"Don't worry. I think they believed me. Just try not to send any lustful, longing glances my way over dinner."

"As if."

"Hey. Could happen. I'm a good-looking, successful guy."

"With an ego the size of Mount Rushmore."

Derek gave her a slow grin and shook his head. "Nope. I won't say it."

"Say what?"

"I hear size matters."

Candy's jaw dropped open, and her gorgeous green eyes went wide. He was going to have to be careful about his own longing, lustful glances over dinner.

6

DESPITE HER DISMISSAL of Derek's joke, longing and lustful thoughts were exactly what Candice was fighting. Of course, the Romeo and Juliet reference was laughable because her interest in Derek was nowhere near that noble. She just wanted his body.

Her father appeared with the tray of chilled martinis. "Hope you like beef, Derek."

"Sure do," said Derek, handing a martini glass to Candice, then taking one for himself.

Her father took his own drink and set the tray down on a sideboard. "Picked myself up some prime steaks in Dallas yesterday."

Derek smiled, nodding appreciatively at the sour-apple martini. "You were in Texas?"

Candice grinned into her glass. Like a lamb to slaughter. Or make that a steer to slaughter.

Her father rocked back on his heels, and she could swear she heard a faint drawl in his voice. "Picked myself up a little spread down there. Hill country. Just outside Abilene."

"You're investing in cattle?" asked Derek.

"Texas longhorns. Breeding ranch. Show stock, mostly."

Derek nodded thoughtfully. "Expect to make a profit, or is it a tax shelter?"

"We fully expect to make a profit."

"Reeves-DuCarter looked at a racehorse once. Decided it was too high of a risk."

"Trick is to know the industry," said Chuck.

Candice nearly choked out a laugh. Her father had studied the industry for exactly two weeks.

"Got one hell of a sire," he continued. "Captain Fantastic. Pedigree back to the eighteen-hundreds. Good conformation, excellent horns."

"Market extend outside of Texas?" asked Derek.

Her father motioned to one of the dinning-table chairs.

Derek pulled out a chair for Candice before he sat down.

Chuck took a chair next to Derek. "All over North America, moving into Europe, too."

Derek nodded. "Interesting prospects."

"Tens of thousands for the right animal."

Her mother joined them at the table as Anna-Leigh served the salad, and her father spent the next hour regaling them with tales of cattle markets and long-horn shows.

Derek didn't once bring up the electronics deal. In fact, he seemed disgustingly interested in the ranch's potential. Probably planning to buy one of his own.

Then, as Anna-Leigh cleared away the dessert and

served coffee, Derek made his move. The sun had already set and storm clouds were billowing on the horizon, cooling the air and moving over the stars.

"Congratulations on the Enoki deal," he said to Candice's father.

He nodded his thanks. "Heard Reeves-DuCarter put in a bid."

"We sure did. Would have dovetailed nicely with our spectrum license." Then he shrugged. "Guess we can't take advantage of that particular investment yet."

Chuck sat forward. "Interested in selling?"

"The spectrum license?"

"Yep."

Derek grinned. "Not a chance."

Chuck glanced at Candice, then back at Derek. "Just friends?"

"Right," said Derek.

"Then you must be here to make a deal."

"That I am," said Derek with another nod.

"Let's get to it, then. What are your terms?"

Derek set down his coffee cup. "You supply the hardware, we supply the infrastructure, we set up proprietary standards and split the profits."

Chuck's eyebrows knit together. He stared hard into Derek's eyes. "Fifty-fifty?"

"Yes."

A slow smile grew on Chuck's face as he sat back in his chair. After a moment's silence, he stuck out his hand. "Done."

"What?" Candice straightened. Just like that? Derek involved with the family business, just like that?

Both men turned to stare at her. Even her mother looked surprised.

She searched her brain for a coherent objection. "Dad, don't you think…I mean, you just got going on the ranch and everything…."

Her father gave her a perplexed look. "Honey, the ranch will wait."

"What do you mean the ranch *will wait?*" He'd just bought the ranch. The ranch was *this* month's project.

Derek nudged her under the table with his knee, shooting her a warning look.

"Is there something about this deal I should know?" her father asked.

Candice opened her mouth. Something he should know? That Derek was sexy? That Derek was tempting? That Derek was dangerous? "I…" She swallowed, her gaze strayed to Derek.

His eyes had hardened to stones.

She squared her shoulders. "I'd hate to see you make a mistake."

"A mistake?" asked her father.

Derek's eye muscle started to twitch.

"You haven't even seen all the details," she pointed out.

Her father reached across the table and covered her hand with his. "Honey, you strike while the iron is hot. Our lawyers can work out the details."

"Right." Derek's voice sounded strained.

DEREK COULDN'T BELIEVE Candy had tried to sabotage his meeting with her father.

As they drew away from her parents' house, the thunderstorm opened above them. He hit the wiper switch and the rhythmic blades penetrated the taut silence inside the car.

Unless she was an incredibly vindictive person, it didn't even make sense. He'd given her everything she wanted on the restaurant contract. And she'd never been directly involved in her father's businesses. Why should she care one way or the other if he and Hammond cut a deal?

He puzzled for several miles while the rain beat down harder and distant lightning strikes lit up the sky.

A few blocks from her house, he realized he couldn't just let it go. He needed to know what she'd been thinking.

He pulled the car to a stop next to Briar Park, hitting the lights and killing the engine. The metallic sound of the rain on the roof increased.

He turned to look at her, stretching an arm over her bucket seat. "Why did you do it?"

She folded her arms across her chest, taking on a mulish expression. "Why'd I do what?"

She knew full well what he was talking about. Lightning flashed and thunder rumbled against the distant coast mountains while he waited.

She remained silent while he stared at her profile.

"Come on, Candy. You don't do obtuse very well."

She turned to look him in the eyes. "Yeah? Well, you don't do intelligent very well."

He ignored that. "What gives? Why'd you undermine me."

She held up her palms. "Hey, I only promised to get you there, I didn't say I'd be a cheerleading squad."

"Cheerleading? I've got news for you, Candy. The introduction wasn't only to provide physical proximity. It also legitimized my proposal. Your endorsement was a very big part of our deal."

She stared at him in silence. A look of remorse might have crossed her face, but it was too dark to tell. "He said yes, Derek."

"I know that."

"So, who cares how you got there?"

"I'm curious, Candy."

"Tough." She reached for the door handle, pushed it open, and stepped into the rain.

"Don't be such an—" he began, but she slammed the door and headed across the park.

Derek swore. He pulled the key from the ignition, pushed open his own door and took off after her.

"Go away," she said as soon as he caught up to her.

"You're getting soaked."

"I won't melt."

"Well, you're sure not walking across the park alone."

"It's not that late."

"It's past ten o'clock."

"Nobody's out in the rain. I'll be fine."

They walked along an oak-lined pathway, approaching a rock garden and the duck pond. The parking-lot lights barely reached them, and it was even darker up ahead. Yeah, like he was going to leave her alone out here.

She picked up her pace. "You got what you wanted. Now back off."

"Tell me why you cared?" he pressed.

She didn't answer, just kept marching. She angled off the pathway and onto the sopping grass. Her shoes had to be soaked through and the raindrops were darkening her little jacket. His white shirt was plastered to his skin. If he'd thought to grab his coat, he could have offered it to her.

"Must be something pretty upsetting," he ventured. "To drag you out here in the rain and the dark."

"What part of 'go away' didn't you understand?"

"What part of 'deal's a deal' didn't you understand?"

She stopped and turned to face him, streaming out a heavy sigh. "Deal's done, Derek."

She had a point. He should shut up, walk her home, and get out of her life. But something wasn't right here, and he'd been bit on the butt too many times by little somethings that weren't right....

"You're not going to try to change his mind, are you?" he asked.

"Please."

"That wasn't exactly a no, Candy."

"What makes you think I could?"

Derek shrugged. "Daddy's little girl… Who knows what you might say to make him distrust me…."

Lightning flashed, illuminating her damp face. "You must have a pretty poor opinion of me."

He lowered his voice. "I don't like things I don't understand, Candy. You were very angry with me when you found out Tyler was spying on Jenna."

Candice let out a harsh laugh. "You think I've been obsessed with revenge for three months? Biding my time? Waiting for the right moment to get you?"

"Sure. I would."

"Yeah? Well, I'm not you."

His tone dropped, his gaze took in the goose bumps on the swell of her breasts. "I've noticed."

Her expression faltered. She wiped her wet hair back from her face. "Leave it alone, Derek."

"Leave what alone?"

"This. Us. It's over."

Derek focused on her damp face, the hair that was plastered to her head, the little jacket that clung to her breasts and the rainwater disappearing into her cleavage. "What do you mean *us?*"

She opened her mouth, but then closed it again without speaking.

"What's going on, Candy?"

Her jaw tightened and her eyes narrowed. "What's going on? You were there. You tell me."

Derek blinked. "I was where?"

She rolled her eyes. Then she leaned forward. "Think, Derek. I know it might be tough for you, given the hectic pace of your oh-so-important life, but isn't there a little something in our past that might make it uncomfortable for me to be around you?"

Comprehension flashed through Derek's brain like the lightning strikes on the hills. He drew back. "This is because you kissed me?"

"Give the man a gold star."

She didn't need to be embarrassed about the kisses. He'd been impressed, astounded, amazed. He was still dying here for the want of her.

"They were only kisses," he said.

"Right."

"You don't blow off multimillion-dollar deals over *kisses.*"

She pushed her wet hair back again, gazing up at him through the driving rain—sweet, sexy, vulnerable. Her voice was barely a whisper in the storm. "Of course you don't."

This wasn't about the kisses. It couldn't be about the kisses. He took a step forward, peering at her expression.

Time slowed down as they stared into each other's eyes. He remembered every detail of every second he'd held her. He remembered her feel, her scent, her taste.

But they were both adults. It wasn't anything to get upset about. "They were kisses, Candy."

She clenched her jaw, glaring at him as though he had the intelligence of a mud fence. "It's not what we *did,* Derek...."

Realization slammed through him.

He brought his palm up to cup her cheek. Her skin was wet and cold, and she shivered as he brushed the raindrops with his thumb.

Oh, yeah. He got it now.

It wasn't what they'd done. His voice was barely a rasp. "It's what we wanted to do."

She gave him a shaky nod.

He admired her honesty. And he knew exactly what she meant. Even now, he could feel the heat building between them. Her skin was warming under his hand. A flush moved into her cheeks. Hot, sexual desire pumped through his system.

He swallowed. "We've still got trouble, haven't we, Candy?"

"We've still got trouble."

Derek clenched his fist. He wanted to kiss her, but he wouldn't. He wasn't touching her again without a specific invitation. Because if they got started, then she backed off, he might never recover.

"Question is," he said, steeling all his strength, lobbing the ball into her court. "What do you want to do about it?"

She was silent for a long minute. "Go home."

He stilled, hating himself for the weakness, but he had to know for sure. "Alone?"

She nodded. "Yes."

Derek bit back a primal scream.

TWO WEEKS LATER, at the Lighthouse Restaurant's opening gala, Candice was still telling herself she'd made the right decision. Derek might have looked like a Greek god come to life with his rain-wet shirt plastered against his chest, but no good could have come from inviting him back to her apartment, stripping off his clothes, making love with him until they couldn't stand up....

She caught a glimpse of him on the dance floor and felt a flush cover her body. She had to force herself to look away. He was gorgeous in his retro Laduci suit, even if nothing could beat the visual memory of him soaking wet.

Jenna slid into the seat next to Candice as the band segued into a 1940s Duke Ellington song. The vintage ball gowns began to sway—chiffon, crepe, satin and velvet. Candice was willing to bet most of them were authentic. The Reeves-DuCarter name definitely brought out the who's who of Seattle.

In the forties spirit in her burgundy satin gown, Jenna brandished an unlit cigarette in a six-inch holder and took a sip of her Manhattan.

"Hypothetically speaking," she said to Candice. "Just for the sake of argument. What exactly would be the harm if the two of you *were* to sleep together?"

"Huh?" Candice pulled back in her chair before she remembered the boned bodice in her strapless gown. She winced from the pinch to her ribs.

"You and Derek," said Jenna.

"What about me and Derek?"

"When he's not looking, you stare at him. When you're not looking, he stares at you. When you danced with the mayor, I thought he was going to crush his Scotch glass."

"I don't know what you're talking about."

"Yeah, yeah, yeah." Jenna waved the ridiculous-looking cigarette holder. "I don't know what happened between the two of you that weekend—"

"*Nothing* happened between us."

"—but you sure didn't satisfy that animal lust you've got going."

"You're nuts."

Jenna crossed her arms over the table, leaning in conspiratorially. "He *is* sexy, isn't he?"

Candice pushed her fingertips against her temples and shook her head.

Jenna gazed across the room to the dance floor. "Broad shoulders, square chin, great eyes, and that nice, tight little butt—"

"Stop it!"

"Am I turning you on?"

Actually, Candice had been turned on for weeks. "You're a married woman."

"Doesn't mean I don't notice all the Reeves brothers are sexy. You caught a look at Erin's smile lately?" Jenna waggled her eyebrows.

"Okay," Candice conceded. "So he's sexy."

"Striker?"

"*Derek.*"

Jenna grinned, eyes sparkling in triumph. "Aha."

"He's also a shark," Candice quickly pointed out. "I grew up around men like him. They collect money, toys and notches on their bedposts. I've known to stay away from them since I was seventeen years old."

"*You're* not seventeen."

"*They're* still dangerous."

"So are you. You're a grown woman. And you want him."

Candice couldn't deny it. She was exhausted from denying it to herself and everyone else. "Doesn't mean I'm going to do anything about it."

"Why not?"

"Because he'll chew me up and spit me out."

"You're tougher than you think," said Jenna. "Go dance with him. Then decide."

"Why are you so hot to throw us together?"

"Because you can practically bottle the chemistry between the two of you. Whatever it is you've *almost* got going, you owe it to yourself to experience it at least once."

Candice let her gaze rest on Derek's broad back, seriously in a mood to be convinced. "You think I should?"

"Maybe it'll get him out of your system. You know, like when you've got an intense craving for chocolate? Ignoring it just makes it worse. Give in, tank up, you're good to go for weeks."

Candice hesitated. Like chocolate? Get her fill of Derek and then walk away?

It could work. Maybe she'd be able to sleep again. And if she was *really* lucky, he'd be a lousy lover and she'd be over him for good.

She'd heard that self-centered men made terrible lovers. Maybe Jenna was onto something here.

"You mean, just wander over there and proposition him?" Candice asked slowly.

Jenna grinned. "Yeah."

"Like, hey, Derek. Wanna get lucky?" Candice teased.

Jenna reached forward and brushed a wisp of hair from Candice's forehead, her gaze sweeping over the black tulle-and-sequin dress Candice was wearing. "You are drop-dead gorgeous in that outfit. And if the heat in his eyes is anything to go by, 'hello' ought to work just fine."

Candice adjusted the strapless dress, resting her hand on her bare chest and taking a bracing breath. "Got a mint?"

Jenna opened the clasp on her purse. "Better than that, I've got a room." She pulled out a key.

"I'm not taking your room. Besides, I can't leave the party early," said Candice. "I've got a million things to do."

"What? You're going to proposition him and make him wait?"

She bit her lower lip. "I guess."

Jenna started to laugh. "Tyler will worship the ground you walk on."

"Don't you *dare* tell Tyler."

Jenna handed her a breath mint. "You're no fun at all."

Candice gave her a secretive smile as she stood up. "Want to bet?"

"Go get 'im tiger."

Candice's confidence carried her almost halfway to the dance floor. Then Duke Ellington turned into Glenn Miller, and Derek escorted his partner off the floor.

Suddenly, he was alone and available.

Her confidence flagged. Her stomach clenched and her knees wobbled for a second. Hoo, boy.

The rational side of her brain clicked in.

This is insane. He was tough, self-assured and powerful. Where she had butterflies in her butterflies.

Maybe she should just turn around—walk, no, run back to her table. She came to a stop and started to turn.

"Candice?" It was Derek's voice. A bass so deep it rumbled over her nerve endings.

She pasted on a smile as she turned back to face him. "Hello, Derek."

The orchestra music swelled.

"Dance?" he asked, holding out an arm.

No! "Of course."

He took her hand and led her onto the dance floor, turning her in his arms and stepping into the strains of the waltz.

The back of her dress was laced in a low V all the way to her waist. His index finger brushed the bare skin between the ties. She could feel her pulse respond to his touch. She inhaled and remembered his scent—part musk, part spice.

She felt her bones begin to soften.

He gathered her closer.

"Congratulations," he whispered in her ear.

"On what?"

"I've heard nothing but compliments on the décor all night long."

She smiled in deep satisfaction. "That's good to hear."

"The historical society is beside themselves. Seems hand-knotted Safavid's are true to the period."

"I know."

"They're taking photos of the chandelier."

Candice's smile grew wider. "Hard to believe you ever doubted me."

He chuckled. "Hard to believe."

He pressed his warm palm against her spine, swirling her in wider circles around the dance floor. His steps were practiced and sure, and she had no trouble following his lead.

She suddenly imagined him naked. His strong arms holding her against his broad chest. The vision was enticing, compelling, like rich chocolate.

Should she ask him?

Could she ask him?

"So, what's next?" he asked.

She tipped her head to look up at him. "Next?"

He nodded.

"You mean after the dance?"

He smiled. "Oh, Candy." Then he touched his

forehead to hers. "I meant after the renovation. What's your next contract?"

"Oh."

"But let's get back to after the dance."

"I can't leave the party early."

Derek hesitated, eyes dark and unfathomable. Then he spoke slowly. "Okay."

They danced in silence to the end of the song.

As the strains drifted away, Derek pulled her close. "I'm dying here, babe. You can't leave me hanging like that."

She closed her eyes, leaning her cheek against his chest. "Later?" She let the tone elaborate on the word.

She felt his chest expand with a rush of air. "Whatever it is you're asking, I'm *positive* my answer is yes. But, Candy…"

Candice tipped her chin to look up at him again, steeling her courage. The renovation was over. She could avoid him after tonight if she put her mind to it.

Like chocolate. She'd have her fill and move on. "You and me. One time. Just to get it out of our systems."

"One *time?*"

She couldn't help a small grin. "One night."

He squinted. "We make love?"

"Right."

"Yes," he rasped. "Absolutely, yes."

7

As Candice stepped back from Derek on the dance floor, the hum in her body notched up a hundred-fold. She couldn't believe she had done it—or rather was going to do it.

A foot apart, their gazes held, breathing in sync.

Candice pointed to the room in general. "I have to…"

Derek nodded. "I know."

She took another step back. "There are people I need to…"

"Go."

"Okay," she said nodding.

"Later."

"Right."

She made her way back to the table in a daze.

"Well?" asked Jenna as Candice sat down.

"I did it."

Jenna let out a little shriek. "You propositioned him?"

Candice nodded. "We're meeting later."

"Well, I'll be damned."

"You didn't think I'd do it?"

"No… Yes…" Jenna grinned. "I'm so proud of you."

"This is a one-shot deal. You'd better keep him away from me after this."

"No problem."

"I'm serious."

"You are a wild woman."

A silly giggle escaped from Candice, and she slapped her hand over her mouth. "I can't believe I did it."

Jenna giggled in return.

"Candice Hammond?"

They both looked up, instantly sobering when they saw it was Myrna West.

"Uh, yes," said Candice, coming to her feet.

The woman held out her hand. "Myrna West from the Seattle Historical Society."

"Of course," said Candice, shaking Myrna's hand. "I heard you speak last month at the chamber of commerce. This is my partner, Jenna Reeves."

"Pleasure to meet you, Jenna."

"Would you like to sit down," Candice offered, quickly moving water glasses out of the way and pulling out one of the leather-upholstered chairs.

"Why, thank you," said Myrna, accepting the seat.

Candice sat down next to her, smoothing her sequined dress in her lap.

"I have to tell you, the board is very impressed with the results you've achieved," said Myrna. "I've been authorized to open discussions on having the Lighthouse designated as a heritage site."

Candice felt her eyes go wide, and a tingle worked its way up her legs. She was momentarily robbed of the power of speech.

Jenna squeezed her hand under the tablecloth.

"We're honored," said Jenna.

Myrna sat back and smiled. "Now normally, we'd approach Derek Reeves, as representative of the owners group. But... Well... As I'm sure you understand, his objectives have not always been in sync with the objectives of the Society."

Candice nodded. That was a polite way of putting it. Altruism wasn't exactly Derek's middle name.

"We're hoping," Myrna continued, "that Canna Interiors might smooth the way for the Society. If you can get Derek to agree to make some changes to the restaurant and formally apply for heritage status, I'll do my best to make sure the board gives the application a favorable hearing."

Candice didn't know what to say. A heritage designation? On their first major contract? It would boost their reputation and open serious doors in the heritage-renovation community. It was a dream come true.

"We'll do our very best," she assured Myrna. "And thank you so much."

Myrna smiled and glanced around the room. "It's lovely. Just lovely."

She stood, and Candice and Jenna stood with her.

"Pinch me," Jenna whispered in Candice's ear as Myrna walked away.

"You pinch *me*," said Candice, sinking back down into her chair. "But how in the heck are we going to convince Derek?"

Jenna dropped back down in her own seat. "Well, you *will* be sleeping with him later tonight…."

Candice froze. Her stomach turned into a block of concrete.

"If you pick the right moment…" Jenna continued.

Panic took over Candice's brain, and her glance flew to where Derek stood talking to his brothers next to the dance floor. "Oh, my, God."

"How can he possibly say no?" asked Jenna.

Candice whimpered, her fists tightening in her lap. "I thought I wasn't going to see him after tonight. Never mind need a favor. Never mind need his cooperation."

Jenna's eyes narrowed. "Hmm."

"What am I going to do?" Candice whispered. "I can't ask him before, or he'll think it's a bribe."

"True," said Jenna.

"I can't ask him after, or he'll think it was—well—a bribe."

"Also true."

"And I can't back out and expect him to ever speak to me again."

"Hmm," said Jenna.

"You're *not* helping."

"It's a problem all right."

"It's a catastrophe."

Jenna gave a decisive nod. "You have to ask him before."

"No way."

"Okay, after."

"Not a chance."

"Then back out."

Candice groaned. She couldn't even imagine Derek's reaction if she backed out. And she didn't want to back out. Her taste buds were all set for chocolate.

"Here he comes," said Jenna.

Candice's heart rate kicked up. "It's too *early*."

A strong, warm hand closed over her bare shoulder.

"The Roosevelt suite," he whispered in her ear, pressing a key into her hand.

Before she could react, he was gone.

"What'd he say?" asked Jenna.

Candice opened her palm. "The Roosevelt suite."

"It's the best," said Jenna, delight shining in her eyes.

"Who *cares?*"

"You have to tell him before," said Jenna. "Just make it clear that the two issues are unrelated."

"Oh, sure. 'Hold that thought, Derek. Before we get naked, there's a little something we need to discuss.'"

Jenna sputtered out a laugh. "Got a better idea?"

Short of divine intervention? Candice had nothing. "The only thing worse than telling him up front would be telling him afterward."

"Or not telling him at all," Jenna pointed out.

"What do you mean, not telling him at all?" Like that was a realistic option.

"I mean, he's leaving."

"Leaving?" Candice twisted around. Sure enough, that was Derek's back heading out the main door.

"Maybe he's going to put the champagne on ice," Jenna suggested.

"The party's not over till midnight."

Jenna straightened and waved. "Tyler?"

"Don't you *dare* tell him a thing," Candice hissed.

"I can be trusted."

Tyler approached the table. "Hey, babe."

"Where did Derek go?"

Tyler snagged Jenna's hand. "I'm ready to dance, and you're asking about my brother? What kind of a wife are you?"

"A curious one."

He pulled Jenna to her feet. "Will satisfying your curiosity be worth my while?"

She winked broadly at him. "You'll never know unless you try."

Tyler nuzzled Jenna's neck. "Looks like I'm a gamblin' man."

"I've always loved that about you."

"Broken water main under the conference wing."

"I didn't know Derek was a plumber," said Jenna.

"They can't get hold of the manager, and they need someone to authorize emergency repairs."

"Will it take long?" asked Candice, hope springing inside her. Could this be divine intervention?

Tyler shrugged. "Might. The emergency repair crew is on the way, but he'll probably need to stick around until they get an estimate."

Candice glanced at her watch. It was nearly eleven. He only needed to stay busy for an hour. Twelve-oh-one, the party would be over, and she'd be out the door.

She'd apologize to him in the morning, then talk to him about the heritage designation *before* they had a chance to make another date.

DEREK HAD the chief financial officer on one cell phone, trying to establish how much of the damage was covered by insurance. He had the conference director on another, trying to set up replacement space for the meetings that were planned for the conference area tomorrow. And he had his eyes on the clock as it ticked over to eleven-fifty-five.

He needed to get back upstairs if he was going to beat Candy to the Roosevelt suite. He'd ordered champagne and strawberries, and chocolate truffles. He doubted they'd get to them before he devoured Candy. But they might be hungry later.

"The city can't get an inspector here for four hours," said the chief financial officer. "But it looks like our maximum exposure for leakage is a five-thousand-dollar deductible and twenty percent."

"On the pipe repair only or consequential damage?" Derek asked into the phone.

"On everything," said the CFO. "And that's the worst-case scenario. If the city's at fault, we're in the clear."

"Gus?" Derek called to the plumbing foreman.

"Yeah?" Gus shouted back above the clank of tools and the roar of water spray.

"Rock and roll. Call in an extra crew. But save the damaged pipe for the inspector."

Gus gave him a quick salute. "You got it."

"The Bayside can give us ten breakout rooms and their mezzanine ballroom for the Remmillard meetings," said the conference director in Derek's other ear. "The ballroom seats five hundred."

The clocked ticked its way toward midnight. "Can you make it work?"

"I'll make it work. You want to alert the Remmillard CEO?"

"You go ahead. But nail down the details first, I don't want him worrying about the caterers all night long."

"Roger." The line went dead.

The clock hit midnight. Derek needed to get out of here.

"You need anything else from me?" he asked the CFO.

"I'll have something for you to sign in the morning."

"Great."

The CFO signed off.

"Hey, Gus," Derek called, stuffing both cell phones into his suit pockets.

"Yeah?"

"You got everything you need?"

As Gus gave him a thumbs-up, the water spray suddenly changed pitch. The foreman jumped backward about five feet, but Derek's reactions weren't as fast.

A plume of water shot across the room, plastering him square, dead center. He could see Gus's grin through the rainbow mist spewing up in front of his eyes.

He bailed to one side. "You want to fix that?" he asked Gus.

"Right, boss."

Derek shook the water from his hands as he headed for the door. Five past twelve and soaked to the skin. Wasn't Candice going to be thrilled to see him?

He squished his way down the double-wide hallway that led to the main lobby. The lobby was quiet, a few late-arriving guests were at the check-in counter. Lights from the line of limousines they'd hired to take the party guests home snaked down the circular driveway.

Derek was glad to see there wasn't a lineup for the cars. At an event like the reopening of the Lighthouse, details like that mattered.

As he watched, a woman stepped into the glass revolving door.

He did a double take.

Candice?

What was *she* doing down here? She had a key to the Roosevelt suite. Why hadn't she used it?

He changed course, striding across the tiled rotunda toward the door. He received a few curious looks from the night staff, but he ignored them.

When he realized she was heading for one of the limos, he increased his pace. He burst through the glass door and onto the sidewalk. *"Candice?"*

She glanced up at him. Her eyes went wide, but she kept going into the back seat of the limousine. "Twenty-two sixteen Westmount Boulevard," she said to the driver.

Derek grabbed the corner of the door before the driver could close it, shouldering the man out of the way. "What are you doing?"

Candice swallowed. "I didn't think you were coming back."

"Not coming *back?*" Was she crazy?

She inched her way across the seat. "You were gone so long. I thought you couldn't make it."

Derek held out his hand to her, stepping to one side. "Of course I made it."

Candice glanced around.

"Come on," said Derek.

"We need to talk," she said.

"We can talk upstairs."

She looked out at him, eyes wide, lips full, Lord help him, she was gorgeous.

"We need to talk before we go upstairs."

"Fine." Derek slid into the limo and closed the door. "Talk."

The purple hued perimeter lights came on. The

driver put it in gear. Derek called, "Wait." But the privacy wall was up, and they glided down the driveway.

This was *not* going according to plan.

"So, talk," he said, trying not to feel annoyed at Candy. He had been gone for over an hour. Who could blame her for wondering if he'd changed his mind?

He loosened his wet tie and yanked it from around his neck. Then he stripped off his sopping jacket and tossed it on one of the other seats. His shoes were ruined, and there probably wasn't any hope for his suit either. His white shirt was plastered to his chest.

Pushing back his wet hair, he turned to look at Candice. He opened his mouth to ask her what it was they needed to talk about, but instead he froze.

She was staring at him like... Well, exactly like he'd fantasized all night. This might not be going according to plan, but they were together, the privacy wall was up and the lights of Seattle were pretty romantic flashing in the tinted windows.

He slid closer, reached out to touch her chin, tipped it up, and his lips descended.

"Derek," she whispered. "We..."

Her voice trailed away as his lips met hers.

Finally. *Finally.*

She was warm and sweet and as soft as spun silk.

He opened his mouth, tipped his head, tunneled his fingers into her hair. The tension of the past two hours instantly evaporated. The roar of the limousine engine faded to a drone, and Candy's soft moans were all that penetrated his brain.

He kissed her neck, making his way across her bare shoulder. Her hands tightened into fists and she dropped her head back.

He whispered her name, worshipped her name. He kissed and tongued and suckled her soft skin, inhaling her scent, wishing time would stand still.

Her fingers went to the buttons on his shirt, fumbling, uncoordinated. He fisted his hand into the fabric and ripped the buttons away, leaving his shirt hanging open. Her fingertips touched his chilled skin, sending tiny impulses into his nervous system.

His body flashed to attention.

His fingers found the tie at the back of her dress and loosened the knot. He pushed the sequined fabric out of the way until it bunched at her waist, exposing her beautiful breasts. He kissed one of her nipples, rolling it with his tongue, glorying in the exquisite sensation of her hot, tender skin.

Her fingertips dug into his scalp, and his name came out on a gasp.

He lowered her to the seat, stripping away her dress, running his index finger under the top of her stockings, plucking at the tiny high-cut panties that barely covered her. Her shoes were forties spiked pumps, the stockings and panties black. Lust thundered through him like a runaway train.

He let his fingertips skim down her flat stomach, watching her jewel-bright eyes as he dipped below the band of her panties. He slid farther, to the searing heat of her body.

Her eyes fluttered closed and he thoroughly kissed her lips. His fingers dipped and delved until her hips came up off the seat.

The limo suddenly stopped.

Derek cursed as Candy gasped in his ear.

He fumbled for the intercom, desperately pressing button after button. It finally crackled to life. "Take us to Bellingham. Then back again."

"Yes, sir," said a crisp, professional voice.

Derek went straight back to kissing her, slipping out of his pants, pushing her panties out of the way, down to her knees, almost to her ankles. Then he gave up on the tangle and kissed his way across her breasts.

Her hands stroked his hair. Her head moved from side to side, small gasps escaping from her lips as her chest expanded and contracted.

Derek ran his fingertips up her thighs, brushing the curls at her apex, finding her tender skin and reveling in the heat.

He couldn't wait any longer.

He quickly donned a condom and position himself over her. "You okay?" he asked.

She scrunched her eyes shut and smiled, reaching down to press his buttocks, pulling him home. He groaned as he slid inside. She fought the tangled panties, until one ankle kicked free, then she wrapped her legs around him.

He plunged into her sweet body, over and over.

The sound of her breathing echoed in his ear, the scent of her skin surrounded him, and he devoured her hot lips in desperate kisses. The streetlights flashed faster and faster in his peripheral vision as the highway hummed beneath them.

She gasped his name, and he moaned hers in return. All sensation in his body coalesced, tightening to unbearable.

"Now?" he rasped

"Now," she answered.

He relinquished control, and heaven rained down around them.

When the last tremors finally died away, and he once again became aware of the whooshing sound of the highway, he lifted her with him, turning onto his back so she straddled him.

"One night?" he asked, wondering how a man could possibly do this only once in his lifetime.

She nodded, pushing into a sitting position. "One night."

He stroked the outsides of her thighs, making his way up her rib cage to the mound of her pert breasts, marveling at how quickly his body was rejuvenating. "Then we'd better not waste it."

Her lips curved into a beautiful smile.

"You're gorgeous," he said.

Her hands went to his chest, fingers spread, wending their way up to his flat nipples. "So are you," she whispered.

"Bellingham is a three-hour round trip."

She bent at the waist, leaning back down to give him a lingering, moist kiss. "Good."

They slowed the pace, making long, leisurely love as the streetlights flashed by on the interstate, first north then south. By the time they hit the traffic of Seattle again, they were covered in a fine sheen of sweat, lying tangled together, gasping for breath.

Derek's limbs tingled. His skin prickled with hypersensitivity. His head felt like a lead weight, and his brain was fogged with pleasure.

"I can honestly say," Candy gasped beside him, "that I am totally and completely satisfied."

Derek reached for her hand, entwining his fingers with hers. "Thank goodness for that." He didn't think his ego could take it if she'd been left unsatisfied. And he sure wasn't up for another round.

Okay, so the spirit was willing, but his body was long past the point of exhaustion.

"We'll be at twenty-two sixteen Westmount Boulevard in five minutes," the driver's voice said over the intercom.

Candice took a deep breath and reached for her dress.

Derek's hand tightened on hers. He wasn't ready to let her go. "You want—"

"I better go." She disentangled her hand.

Derek would have argued, but he didn't want to mar what might very well have been the best night of his life.

CANDICE SHUT HER APARTMENT DOOR and banged her head back against it three times in rapid succession. She was supposed to tell him about the heritage designation *before* she touched him—not during, not after and definitely not *never*.

What was she *thinking?*

Okay, so she knew what she was thinking: that Derek in a wet shirt ought to be illegal, and that Derek out of a wet shirt was better than chocolate—*way* better than chocolate.

Thank goodness they'd gone all the way to Bellingham and not just over to Bellevue. An hour wouldn't have been nearly enough time to satisfy her craving.

She dropped her purse, kicked off her shoes and made her way toward the bathtub. On the bright side, she was temporarily over her Derek lust. Maybe now she'd be able to talk to him without fantasizing.

She cranked the taps and poured in some lemongrass bubble bath. She still had to convince him sex hadn't been a bribe for the heritage designation. And she still had to convince him to go for the designation. She knew it was going to be a problem, but she was having a hard time feeling too stressed about anything at the moment.

She peeled off her dress and discarded her underwear. If she stopped by his office tomorrow morning and made it clear that the two issues were unrelated, he *might* believe her.

She sighed as she slipped into the hot sudsy water.

He'd *better* believe her. Because she had no desire to explain to Jenna why she hadn't asked about the heritage designation before having sex with Derek. There were certain details women didn't need to know about their brothers-in-law.

8

THE INTERCOM BUZZED in Derek's office on the top floor of the Reeves-DuCarter building, breaking his hard-won concentration. He looked up from the water inspector's preliminary report and pressed the Talk button.

"Yes, Marion?"

"A Candice Hammond here to see you regarding the Lighthouse Restaurant."

Derek's heart skipped a beat, and page six of the report dropped from his fingertips.

Candy?

Here?

Now?

Had she changed her mind about the one-night rule? Had "one night" meant twenty-four hours? Were they still on the clock?

"Mr. Reeves?"

Derek pulled his ridiculous thoughts up short. He was behaving like a hormone-ravaged teenager. "Uh. Sorry, Marion. Send her in."

He carefully closed the inspector's report and centered it on his cherrywood desktop. He was fine. He was in control. Last night was last night. It was over and done.

But what if they *were* still on the clock?

He jumped up and slipped into his jacket, straightening his tie as he glanced around the room. Sunlight streamed through the glass walls, glaring directly on his guest chairs. He strode to the corner and adjusted the opaque blinds.

He could offer her something from the wet bar, maybe cancel his ten o'clock. They could lock the office door and—

The door whooshed opened, and Candy walked in, looking crisp and professional in a cream-colored jacket and matching skirt. Her blond hair was swept back off her face. Her emerald blouse set off her eyes.

Of its own volition, his gaze worked its way down her figure, dismissing the mannish cut of the clothes, remembering her curves, savoring last night's images, visualizing her naked all over again.

Then Marion closed the door with a firm click, and Candy marched across the carpet toward one of his burgundy leather guest chairs. Her posture was different than he remembered—stiff, no-nonsense.

"Before we get started," she said, voice crisp as the outfit. "I want to make it clear that this has nothing to do with last night."

Derek's mood flagged. So much for locking the office door. "Nothing?"

She shook her head, bracing her hands on the back of his chair.

He swallowed his disappointment, forcing a neutral tone to his voice. "Please, sit down."

As she sat, he lowered himself into his own chair.

She smoothed her hands over a manila envelope in her lap. "I have a proposition for you."

Yes!

Maybe.

He clenched his jaw, forcing himself to pick up his pen and nod thoughtfully. Odds were that her proposition didn't bear any resemblance to the one he had in mind. The one where they really did take off to that tropical island together and get naked for a month.

He squared his shoulders and pasted on his best shark expression. "What can I do for you?"

Candy took a deep breath. She looked him in the eye for a moment, then her gaze shifted nervously to a point beside his left ear and she smoothed the envelope three times with the palms of her hands.

Whatever she was about to say couldn't be good.

"Myrna West from the Seattle Historical Society has contacted me regarding a heritage designation for the Lighthouse," she said.

Derek's forehead tightened as the words penetrated. His eyebrows rose. He'd had experience with the indomitable Ms. West and her idealistic cronies. If she had her way, the entire city would be preserved for posterity.

He had to hand it to Myrna, approaching Candy

was much smarter than approaching him straight on. It would take some pretty fast talking to get him to listen to a proposal from the Historical Society.

His mind started clicking through Myrna's possible agendas, then it clicked through Candice's likely interests. When he started adding up the timetable, he stilled. "When?"

Her gaze darted back to his eyes. "What?"

"*When* did Myrna West contact you?"

"Last night."

His stomach clenched. Myrna offered up a heritage designation, and suddenly Candy was all over him in the back of the limo?

Coincidence?

Not likely.

He felt a sudden shot of betrayal.

But he ruthlessly squelched it.

He'd had mind-blowing sex with a woman he'd been fantasizing about for months. Why should he care one way or the other how they'd got there?

She wanted to bargain with her body? Okay by him. Just so long as he was the guy she was bargaining with.

Candy's lips compressed. "One has nothing to do with the other, Derek."

Right. Like he was going to buy that.

"*Noth-thing*," she repeated, drawing out each syllable, staring hard into his eyes.

"Well, if it does," he drawled, "you definitely miscalculated."

Her brow furrowed. "Wha…" Then she shook her head, obviously regrouping. "Never mind. I—that is, Jenna and I think a heritage designation would benefit the hotel."

"You don't want to know why you miscalculated?"

"No."

"Why not?"

"The answer to that question can't be complimentary."

What was she talking about? "You were there, Candy."

"*Derek.*"

"Do you honestly think—"

"Can we talk about the heritage designation?"

Derek didn't want to talk about the heritage designation. He wanted to talk about last night. More particularly, he wanted to talk about it in the context of tonight, and tomorrow night and the night after that.

"Please?" she asked.

Derek tossed the pen down onto the desk. "Fine."

She straightened. "Jenna and I think an increased customer base would result—"

"Are you still fully satisfied?"

Her eyes flashed. "Derek!"

"Because, well, I gotta say that—"

"Will you *stop?*"

No he wouldn't stop. Not until he figured this out. Not until he had his answers. Not until he'd exhausted *every* possible chance they'd make love again.

He opened his mouth. Then he closed it.

What the hell was he doing? Sure she was a babe. But there were lots of babes out there. He was in control—of the situation, of himself, of his emotions.

He forced his shoulders to relax, and he unclenched his fists. He was *in* control. "Right. Sorry."

She drew in a deep breath. "A heritage designation could increase your customer base—"

"No, it won't."

"Will you *please* give me time to finish?"

Despite himself, Derek felt the corners of his mouth twitch. It was on the tip of his tongue to remind her that she'd *finished* last night and then some.

Candice threw up her hands. "Will you *stop*..."

"I didn't say a word."

She closed her eyes for a second. "Okay. Fine. You're right. You didn't."

She leaned forward, pinning him with a schoolmarm gaze that all but dared him to mess up again. "A heritage designation will help establish Reeves-DuCarter's reputation as a good corporate citizen. There are many arts and community groups who use heritage buildings for their functions. You could get their business. That would help the hotel become a society landmark, and you could piggyback a publicity campaign onto the certification."

It was an eloquent argument, an impassioned argument. "What's in it for you?"

"What do you mean?"

"Not that I don't think you're a purely civic-minded philanthropist, but it must be good for Canna Interiors." Derek relaxed. He was back on his game, looking at the angles, speculating on her motivation.

Candice squared her shoulders and crossed her legs. "Our long-term goal is to specialize in heritage buildings. Naturally, having our first major renovation certified would be a coup and would raise the credibility of the firm."

"Why didn't you just say so?"

"I did."

Derek waved a hand. "Forget all the song and dance about it being good for me. Why not just tell me it's good for you and ask me to cooperate?"

Candice stared at him in puzzlement. "What? You'd do it for Jenna? Because she's family?"

"Why couldn't I do it for you?"

"Why?"

"Maybe I'm a nice guy."

Her eyes narrowed tighter and she cocked her head. "What…"

Derek gave up. "How much will it cost?"

She reached out and slid the envelope across the desk. "Here's a preliminary estimate."

He pulled out the sheaf of paper, glancing at the list of figures. "Getting a heritage designation isn't a good economic move—"

"But—"

"A good corporate citizen move? Maybe. Could

we dovetail some advertising and community good-will? Possibly. But I'd have to be a nice guy to say yes to this, Candice." His gaze swept down to the bottom line. "A *really* nice guy. You think I'm a nice guy?"

After a long pause, she spoke slowly. "You're not as bad as I thought you were."

Derek looked up in time to catch the small smirk at the corners of her mouth.

He held her gaze, telling himself he had to do it. "And you're better than I ever dreamed."

She quickly looked away. "Derek."

He shook his head, his turn to smirk. "I warn you, and I warn you…" He waited, but she didn't meet his eyes.

He cleared his throat. "You know, I don't have any time to spend—"

Her gaze snapped back. "I promise, it won't take much of your time. I can do the historical research, put together the proposal, make all the logistical arrangements…." Her cheeks were flushed, her expression hopeful, her lips soft.

Derek slid the envelope back across the desk.

Making a decision based on emotion was *never* a good idea. Making a decision based on a pair of legs, jewel-bright eyes and a lingering afterglow was even worse.

It wasn't like he didn't have a million crises to deal with, and he was sure this heritage thing was going to cost him plenty. But he was weak when it came to Candy. Embarrassingly weak.

He was going to regret this.

"Go for it," he said.

Her amazing eyes lit up the room, and her smile shot all the way to his toes.

Regret was the last thing on his mind.

"THEY'RE GOING TO *WHAT*?" asked Striker.

"Try for a heritage designation," answered Derek, covering his embarrassment with a swig of his beer. He'd had a few hours of sober second, third and fourth thoughts on this.

He and his two brothers were watching the sunset over Puget Sound from Derek's deck. It wasn't exactly boys' night out, but it was the closest thing they could muster lately.

"Since when did the Quayside go all artsy-fartsy?" asked Striker.

"They're not artists, they're heritage curators," explained Derek, knowing full well it didn't matter what name he gave them or how he rationalized the decision, this was going to raise eyebrows on the board members.

"Well, excuse me." Striker glanced at Tyler for support.

Tyler leaned back in his deck chair, rocking it up on two legs. "Don't look at me. If Jenna's happy, I'm happy."

Striker gave a reluctant nod. "Fine. So Jenna's happy. My life's great when Erin's happy. But what the hell's in this for Derek?"

Tyler's slow grin widened until he looked like a Cheshire cat. "Excellent question, bro." He turned his attention to Derek. "Tell us, Derek. What's in it for you?"

Derek bought himself a few seconds by letting his gaze scan the freshly trimmed lawn that ran from his deck to the rocky beach. "The satisfaction of knowing I'm a good corporate citizen who's helping to keep Seattle's history alive."

Striker coughed out an incredulous laugh.

"Is that what you were doing last night?" asked Tyler, voice laced with a knowing snicker. "Helping to keep Seattle's history alive?"

Derek shot a glare at his brother.

Striker sat up straighter in his deck chair. "Hello? What did I miss?"

"Derek's reason for becoming a good corporate citizen," said Tyler.

Striker glanced from one brother to the other. "Yeah?"

Derek clamped his jaw shut, not about to fess up to a thing.

Tyler showed no such compunction. "After the party last night, Derek and Candice—"

"Whoa. Candice told *Jenna?*" Now that threw Derek.

Tyler grinned.

Derek swore.

"Well, somebody better tell *me,*" said Striker.

"It was nothing," said Derek.

Tyler's eyebrow arched. "Nothing."

"We went for a limo ride."

"In a *limo?*" asked Striker, a note of admiration in his tone. "That's one up on me."

"It was nothing," said Derek.

"That's not what I'm hearing," said Tyler.

"Nothing I haven't done with a dozen other women." Now that was a bald-faced lie. Derek hadn't come anywhere close to that with any other woman.

"I'm hearing—"

"I don't care *what* Jenna told you."

Tyler grinned smugly as he took another swig of his beer. "Jenna didn't tell me anything. I was fishing."

Striker burst out laughing.

Derek's stomach clenched. He hated it when his baby brother pulled one over on him. But he kept his face poker-straight. "Then I take it all back."

Striker whistled through his teeth. "The back of a limo."

Derek lifted his beer bottle, holding out his index finger and pointing at each of his brothers. "I don't want *either* of your wives hearing about this." Candy didn't deserve to be gossiped about.

"Let me get this straight. You boff her—"

"Striker…" Derek growled.

Striker cleared his throat. "Excuse me. You *go for a limo ride* with Candice. A really *fun* limo ride. And the next morning you agree to become Seattle's citizen of the month?"

Striker looked at Tyler, and Tyler looked at Striker.

"He's toast," said Tyler.

"Crispy," said Striker.

"It's not like that," said Derek.

They both coughed out a laugh.

Derek shook his head and finished the dregs of his beer. It wasn't like that.

Other companies did this kind of thing all the time. Candy had made some good points. They'd get significant PR out of the heritage designation. And she was doing all the work. He just had to sign a few papers, spend a little more money and then he was done.

Striker stood up. "Much as I love discussing Derek's sex life, I gotta take off. There's a sweet young bride waiting at my house."

"Mine, too," Tyler agreed. "Think I'll pump her for information about Candice—"

"Don't—" Derek began, then he caught the look on his brother's face. Tyler was yanking his chain again.

As his brothers headed around the house to their cars, their low conversation was punctuated by breaks of laughter. Derek didn't even want to know what they were discussing.

He cleared the deck, straightened the kitchen, then sat down at his desk, determined to put in a couple of hours' work before bed. By eleven o'clock he'd given up on trying to grasp the schematics for a new cell phone design, and he hit the lights and headed upstairs.

Sitting on the edge of his bed, his mind flashed back twenty-four hours. Once again, he saw Candy's eyes, her smile, her honey-toned body. He vividly remembered her taste and her scent, and the feel of her curvy body pressed tight against his own.

He wondered what she was doing right now.

Asleep? Awake?

Had she thought about him at all?

His gaze shifted to his telephone. He'd always had a great memory for numbers, and hers flashed through his brain. He watched with a measure of amazement as his hand reached for the receiver and his index finger punched in the number.

She picked up on the second ring, voice husky and sleepy. "Hello?"

He resisted the urge to ask what she was wearing.

"For the record," he said.

"Derek?"

"Your miscalculation? It was in *not* asking me for the heritage designation while we were in the limo."

There was a silent pause. "Why?"

"Because, at that point, I would have agreed to anything."

"You agreed to it anyway."

She had him there.

There was another long silence. He could think of a million things he wanted to say, from the lightly sarcastic to the downright erotic.

Instead, he closed his eyes and let out a breath. "Good night, Candy."

"Good night, Derek."

CANDICE HAD PUZZLED over Derek's words all night long. He would have agreed to anything *before* they made love or *after* they made love? Did he mean she was good, or just that he'd wanted it really bad?

She was no closer to an answer as she followed Jenna into the manager's office in the Quayside Hotel. It had seemed like a good place to start their search for historic information.

"You know, this is the first place Tyler ever kissed me," said Jenna as she rattled her way into Henry Wenchel's file drawer, searching for the original architectural drawings.

"You mean the time you got all paranoid and thought he wasn't attracted to you?" she asked Jenna.

"That's the time," said Jenna, smiling as she retrieved a thick file of papers. "It was while we were looking at these."

She closed the file drawer, straightened and headed for Henry's desk, spreading out the crackling, yellowed drawings.

Candice flipped on the desk lamp and helped Jenna smooth the corners of the sheets. "These are great," she breathed, peering down at the faint printing of the circa 1940 architectural drawings.

They flipped through the pages, finding the original floor plan, the elevation views and handwritten notes from the architect.

"So where were you the first time Derek kissed you?" asked Jenna.

"We need to frame these," said Candice, not wanting to remember Derek's kisses, his scent, his deep voice or anything else about him at the moment.

Jenna elbowed her playfully in the ribs. "Give."

"In the Tunnel of Love," said Candice. "I told you that months ago. Maybe we could hang some of them in the restaurant after we make the presentation."

"That one didn't count," said Jenna.

"Look. Here's where they added the conference wing."

"Interesting," said Jenna. "Where did he first *really* kiss you."

"On the mouth. Did you know the hotel had a basement?"

"They renovated most of it for parking about twenty-five years ago. And I meant the geographical location, not the anatomical position."

"Anything left down there?"

Jenna grinned, stepping back to cross her arms over her chest. "Yeah. And I know how to get there. But, now that we're alone, you have to dish. Start with where Derek first kissed you."

Candice began sorting out the best drawings to take to the framing shop. "You are way too nosy."

"I heard it was in the limousine."

"Who told you about the limousine?"

"Is it true?"

"No."

"Tyler told me about the limousine. Guess he got it from Derek. What happened to the Roosevelt suite?"

Derek had bragged to Tyler? Why would he do that? He was thirty-four not sixteen.

Not that she minded Jenna knowing a few details. In fact she was surprised Jenna had waited a full day to corner her. What Candice didn't like was becoming a topic of general discussion. "You know, that Reeves-DuCarter family is *way* too interested in each other's sex lives."

Jenna blinked. "You had *sex* in the limo?"

"See that, their voyeurism is rubbing off on you."

"No. You're rubbing off on me. Face it, you couldn't wait to get the details on me and Tyler."

"Different set of circumstances," said Candice. "Tyler was a relationship. Derek is merely chocolate." *Chocolate*, she reminded herself—delicious, but fleeting, and too much of it was bad for your health.

"If you'll recall, Tyler started off as my fling to obliterate Brandon."

"Worked, too, didn't it?" Candice held up one of the drawings, firmly focusing on the history of the hotel. The lines on the drawing were a bit faint, but they were legible. "I think we should preserve them just the way they are."

"We're not talking about me," said Jenna.

Candice let out a mock sigh. "We're *talking* about the heritage designation."

"No, we're talking about what happened after you and Derek left the party."

"You're not going to back off unless I give, are you?"

"Would you?"

Candice rolled up the chosen plans and slipped them into a cardboard tube. Best thing to do was get this over with quick. That way she could banish Derek from her brain for the rest of the day.

"Okay, here's the dirt. He kissed me in the Lighthouse the weekend Tyler locked us up there. And yes, we had wild sex in the back of the limo."

Jenna looked impressed. "With the driver there and everything?"

"The privacy wall was up."

"Oh." Now Jenna looked disappointed.

"What? You're an exhibitionist?"

"No. But I am damned impressed."

Candice allowed herself a quick, furtive memory. "Twice."

"Really?"

"Uh-huh."

"Going to do it again?"

Candice stuffed the cardboard tube under her arm. "Nope. Like chocolate, remember? I've had my fill."

"So that's it?"

Candice switched off the desk lamp. "Absolutely."

"How long you go between chocolate cravings anyway?"

"Few months."

"I give you a few days."

Quite frankly, it had only taken a few hours. But Candice wasn't about to crack. It was one thing to sleep with Derek when she thought it would solve her problem of obsessing about him. But she couldn't go around having sex with him every few days just to keep her psyche on an even keel.

He was still danger with a capital *D*.

"You'd lose," she said to Jenna, folding the remaining drawings.

"We'll see," said Jenna.

Candice took the leftover drawings back to the file drawer. "How do I get to the basement?"

The office door opened and Tyler appeared.

"Through the spa," said Jenna. "There's a door from the garden."

"A door from the garden to what?" asked Tyler.

"The basement," said Jenna.

Tyler grinned as he strode into the room. "Ahh. The basement. That's where we lock up the bodies."

"Any of those bodies from 1940?" asked Candice. "The more artifacts we can present to the Historical Society the better."

Tyler wrapped an arm around Jenna's waist. "I'm sure there are. The Elliots owned the building back then. Gambling, extortion, infidelity. They must have committed a murder or two." He pulled Jenna back into the cradle of his thighs. "This office bring back any memories, babe?"

Jenna smacked his hand. "Behave. You're a married man."

Candice pointed at the door with her thumb, joking, since Henry was due back any minute. "You two want me to make myself scarce?"

"Yes," said Tyler.

"No," said Jenna. She tipped her head back to look up at him. "There's something wrong with you."

"True. But you've got the cure."

"Can you get us into the basement?" asked Candice.

"Don't have the key. Derek does though."

Candice shivered at the thought of seeing Derek again. If it were a shiver of fright, she wouldn't have been worried. But it was a shiver of anticipation, excitement even. This was *not* good.

"Think you could get it from him?" she asked Tyler.

Tyler shook his head. "Got a meeting in ten minutes."

Candice gave Jenna a hopeful look. "You?"

Jenna shrugged apologetically. "I've got a meeting on the library proposal."

Candice swore under her breath. "I promised Derek I wasn't going to bother him with the research."

"But you're willing to send us in to bother him?" asked Tyler.

"You're family," said Candice.

"She's ruthless," Tyler said to Jenna.

Candice considered her options. "Does the security office have a key?"

Tyler shrugged. "They must have one somewhere. But they're not going to let you go down there without Derek's permission."

Jenna touched Candice's arm, her voice full of falsely inflated compassion. "Don't worry. If you did it in a limo, you can do it in the basement, too."

Candice's face heated.

Tyler held up his palms. "Hey, I don't know nuthin'."

She shook her head. "I knew there was a reason we Hammonds stayed away from you Reeves-DuCarters all these years."

9

CANDICE WAS STAYING WELL AWAY from a certain Reeves-DuCarter for the foreseeable future. She figured if she hurried, she could be in and out of the basement before anybody noticed.

She made it into the spa without any trouble. And then she made it safely into the garden. And it didn't take long to spot the concrete staircase leading to an old basement door.

Perfect. All she had to do was casually make her way past the potted ferns, flower beds and cedar hedges, slip down the stairs and jimmy the lock with her credit card. She'd seen it done a million times on television. How strong was the lock likely to be, considering the door was accessed through an interior garden?

She strolled past a young couple sitting on one of the wooden benches. A pair of elderly women smiled at her as they admired the late-blooming roses. She took a quick look over her shoulder and through the glass wall of the spa. Nobody seemed to be paying any attention to her, so she scooted down the stairs.

The temperature cooled as she descended into the damp concrete stairwell. The cement was chipped and cracked in places, and fuzzy moss had crept along the dark corners. An old wooden-plank door was crossed with iron supports and held shut by a sliding metal bolt. The bolt was held in place by a rusty padlock. And she was in luck. The lock had been left hanging open.

With a final glance back up at the garden, she wriggled the lock from the latch and worked the bolt through the holes. With a creak and a groan, the big door yawned inward.

Bingo.

If this decorating gig didn't work out, maybe she could join the CIA.

She felt around the end of the wall, quickly locating a light switch. She held her breath and flicked it up. Fluorescent lights buzzed to life, slowly sheeting the big room with white light. She walked down the three wooden stairs that led to floor level and pushed the door closed behind her.

The high ceiling was a crisscross of water pipes and electrical wiring. Huge water boilers stood to one side, obviously no longer in use, since they were still, cold and quiet. Candice rubbed her chilled arms as she took a few steps across the concrete.

She peered through the first doorway into a darkened room. Again, it was easy to find the light switch, and she turned on the lights. It was the old laundry room, full of industrial washers and dryers. Clotheslines were strung at intervals across the ceiling. But there was nothing of historical significance.

She continued down the wide corridor, discovering staff washrooms and changing rooms, a service ramp and an electrical room.

Just when she thought she'd come away empty-handed, she discovered a bank of white closet doors at the far end of the hallway. She opened the first one to reveal a row of maid uniforms. They were dusty, but in surprisingly good condition. On the shelf above were starched caps, and on the floor below, pairs of shoes still attached together by plastic straps and marked with their sizes.

Candice smiled, leaving the door open as she moved onto the next closet. There she found bottles of bleach, liquid cleaner, brooms and mops.

Next, she discovered a stack of old menus, and her brain snapped to attention. Not only were the menus artifacts, but the chef might consider using them to come up with some "retro-specials" for the current restaurant.

Her brain humming with ideas for incorporating the historic menu, she turned her attention to the shelf below. There she found a thick leather-bound book. She picked it up and let out a little shriek of excitement.

It was a hotel register.

She crouched down on one knee, peering into the depths of the shelf and finding a whole stack of hotel registers. Scanning the dates, she discovered they were from the earliest days of the Quayside. There was no telling who had stayed here.

"Stand up slowly," said a man's voice behind her, "and step away from the cabinet."

Candice's stomach lurched. She quickly swiveled on the balls of her feet to see a young security guard, one hand on his holstered gun, the other pointing at her.

"Ma'am," he said. "I'm going to have to ask you to put down the book, and step away—"

"You don't understand." Candice shook her head as she slowly rose. "I work here. I was just—"

"May I see some ID?" he asked.

She straightened. "Of course."

"Put the book down, please."

"Right." She set it back down on the shelf and opened her purse.

"Slowly," he said, eyeing her with suspicion.

She forced a friendly smile as she hunted for her wallet. "There's a perfectly logical explanation for this. I'm doing a historical report on the hotel, and—"

"Just the ID for now, ma'am."

She pulled out her driver's license and held it out to him.

He took it from her hand, glancing down at her picture. "This is your driver's license."

"Right."

"I'll need your hotel ID."

"Oh. No. You don't understand. I'm not actually an employee. I'm a con—"

"You'd better come with me." He took a step to one side and gestured for her to precede him.

"But…" She looked longingly back at the open cupboards. She didn't want to let the guest registers out of her sight.

"This way, please."

"There are plenty of people who can vouch for me."

"We'll call them when we get to the security office." He picked up his walkie-talkie. "John? Got an intruder in the basement. I'm bringing her up. You want to contact the police?"

The police? Now Candice was getting annoyed. "I'm *not* an intruder. I was hired by Henry Wenchel."

The security guard raised his eyebrows and gestured toward the door.

She pointed to the walkie-talkie. "Call Henry on that thing. He'll tell you who I am."

The security guard's expression and the tone of his voice made it clear he didn't believe her. "We can call *Henry* from upstairs."

She couldn't keep the sarcasm from her own voice. "You mean after they cuff me?"

"Ma'am." He gestured again.

Candice shook her head, taking a frustrated breath as she marched for the door. She didn't need this. She'd discovered a treasure trove, and she couldn't wait to see what else was hiding in the cabinets.

The security guard fell into step behind her, sticking close, as if he expected her to bolt. Yeah. She was a mastermind criminal about to rip them off for some cleaning supplies and vintage maid uniforms. That made *such* good sense.

She kept her head high, trying not to feel self-conscious as she crossed the spa and the lobby. As far as any of the guests knew, she and the nice security guard were talking about decorating his office. They had no way of knowing she was practically under arrest.

Still, she squirmed every time somebody's gaze rested on her.

She was grateful when they finally made it to the security office. That is, until he sat her in a chair in a little back room, left her there alone and locked the door behind him.

She jumped up and shouted through the door. "Call Henry Wenchel."

Then she sat back down in the hard chair and rested her head in her hands. This was all going to be resolved in a few minutes, she told herself. Sure, it had been embarrassing, but the security guard was the one who'd feel stupid once Henry confirmed who she was.

She couldn't imagine anyone making a big deal about the fact that she hadn't had formal permission to go down to the basement. She'd had free run of the hotel for weeks now. It wasn't like she'd even broken a lock.

The door opened again, and the security guard stepped back in.

Thank goodness.

"—don't know what she was doing down there,"

he said as two uniformed police officers filed in behind him. "What with the ambassador's upcoming stay, I didn't want to take any chances."

The ambassador? What ambassador?

"Did you call Henry?" she asked.

"Henry's unavailable," said the security guard.

The police officers closed the door behind them, standing shoulder to shoulder in the tiny room. "Mind if we ask you a few questions, ma'am?"

Candice was beginning to hate the word *ma'am*. It conveyed such false respect. She kept her attention on the security guard, pretending the cops weren't there. "Can you call Tyler Reeves? He knows who I am."

"Why don't you answer our questions first," said one of the officers, pulling out a notebook.

She switched her gaze to him. "Because if one of you calls Tyler Reeves, there won't be any need for questions."

"What were you doing in the basement?" asked the second officer.

Candice couldn't decide whether to answer the stupid questions or remain mulishly silent until somebody did the right thing. She glanced from cop to security guard to cop. "I was researching a project on the history of the hotel."

The cop jotted down some notes.

"And this project," he said, "it was for…"

Candice paused. She wasn't sure if she should say anything about the heritage designation. The security guard might leak it to the other staff. If the information was made public before the announcement, it would dilute the impact of any PR campaign.

"We can ask these same questions downtown," said the other cop.

Before she could respond, the door to the little office opened, and the security guard was forced to step quickly to one side and hunch his shoulders while he hugged the wall.

Derek filled the doorway.

Suddenly going downtown didn't look so bad.

He glanced around the room, gaze coming to rest on Candice.

"I can take it from here," he said to the cops. Then he smiled affably and held out his hand to each of them. "Thanks for responding so quickly."

"You know this woman?" asked the cop with the notepad.

"I know her," said Derek, and the security guard paled a little.

The cops both tipped their hats and left the office.

Derek turned to the security guard, again holding out his hand. "Good work."

The security guard visibly relaxed.

"But she's legit," said Derek.

The man tensed again. "I'm very—"

"Not a problem," said Derek, clapping the man on the shoulder. "You did your job." Then he opened the door, and the security guard quickly took his cue.

Derek clicked the door shut, leaning back against

it. He grinned broadly, and it was obvious he was trying not to laugh.

Candice wasn't feeling nearly so jovial about the whole thing. "You *did your job?*" she mimicked.

"He did," said Derek. "You expect him to ignore a strange woman poking around in an abandoned basement? You could have been setting explosives."

"I was reading old menus."

"He had no way of knowing that."

"Well he could have checked the facts before calling in the cavalry. I thought they were going to cuff me and haul me downtown."

Derek took a step forward. "I'd have bailed you out."

Candice stood up. Their height difference was bad enough without her sitting on a chair. "Thanks so much."

"What were you doing down there?"

"I was looking for historical information and artifacts for the presentation."

"Find anything?"

"Yes." Candice pushed the humiliation of the last half hour out of her mind. She was still thrilled with her discovery. "I found the original guest registers. I want to get back down there."

"Then, let's go."

"What do you mean, let's go?"

"I mean, I'll come with you. That way you won't get yourself arrested again."

"I didn't get arrested."

"Almost." He looked her up and down, his grin widening. "I should have waited until they got the cuffs out."

"Pervert."

His eyes lit up. "You know it."

Candice ignored the little thrill that rushed along her bloodstream. "Don't you have important things to do?"

"Nope."

"You must have a meeting? A conference? Something to sign?"

"None of the above."

"I thought you were a busy and important man?"

"You caught me in a lull." He opened the door. "Let's go search the basement."

WITH CANDICE HEADING down the hall in front of him, Derek pulled out his cell phone and sent a quick text message to his secretary, telling her to cancel his three o'clock meeting. He wasn't comfortable letting Candice stumble around the old basement by herself— hotel liability if nothing else.

He flipped the phone shut, stuffed it back in his suit pocket, and caught up to her. "So what's your approach?"

She glanced up. "Hunt around in the basement until I find stuff that's interesting."

"I meant your approach to the presentation. You must have a theme in mind."

Her eyes narrowed. "Why do you want to know?"

They descended the mezzanine stairs to the main lobby. A long lineup stretched from the check-in counter, and Derek automatically checked to see that all of the stations were manned. They were.

"Because it's my building, my restaurant. Am I not allowed to ask questions?"

She still looked suspicious as they headed across the lobby to the spa entrance. "I thought you were leaving the project to me?"

"I changed my mind."

"But—"

"I'm joking, Candy. I won't get in your way. I'm just curious about how it's going."

She opened the spa door, and he grabbed it from the top, holding it ajar while she walked through. The temperature and humidity immediately rose as they left the lobby behind.

"I haven't decided on a theme," she said, her enthusiasm obviously overcoming her reluctance to talk to him. "When I found the menus, I thought we could focus on the fashion styles of the day, maybe find some information on the social life around lavish dinner parties."

Derek stuck close as she negotiated around the whirlpool tubs on her way to the garden door.

"But then I found the guest register, and how many famous people had stayed here. We might be able come up with something spectacular if we researched notable guests."

Derek nodded. It had flash. It had pizzazz. Marketing would latch on to tales of famous, or infamous, guests.

He scooted past her to open the garden door and hold it for her. "I like it."

She glanced up. "You do?"

"Yes. It's good. Have you thought about talking to Marco Elliot?"

"Who?"

"Marco Elliot. My family bought the hotel from his family in the midsixties. They were the original owners."

Candice looked instantly interested. "And he's still alive?"

"He's forty-five. The grandson of the man who built the Quayside."

Candice nodded. "I'll definitely talk to him."

As they came to the basement staircase, Derek put a hand on her arm. "Hold on a second."

"What's wrong?"

He pulled out his cell phone. "I'm going to call him before we go down. Reception's better out here."

"Just like that?" she asked.

He punched the number pad. "Just like that."

"You know his number?"

Derek tapped his skull. "Mind like a steel trap."

"That's amazing."

"I'm an amazing guy."

The receptionist picked up.

"Marco Elliot, please. It's Derek Reeves calling."

"One moment please, Mr. Reeves."

Candice watched him, and he watched her right back. Her hair seemed to sparkle in the afternoon sun. Her complexion was spring-fresh, her features delicate. He'd battled hard to keep his memories at bay, but right now their night together danced through his head in exquisite detail.

The line clicked and the elevator music ended. "Hey, Derek. How's it going?"

"Hi, Marco. It's good. Everything's just great. How about you?"

"Profits are up. Overhead is down. I'm a little worried about world metal prices, but what can you do?"

Derek chuckled. "You be able to squeeze me in for a drink this afternoon?"

Candice's eyes widened at his words. The expression reminded Derek of her orgasms, and he felt himself slide back into the memory.

"No problem," said Marco. "After four work for you?"

"Perfect," said Derek, his voice huskier than he'd intended. He cleared his throat.

"What are you—" Candice began.

Derek held up a finger to keep her quiet.

"The Sea Shanty sound good?" he asked Marro.

"Margarita night," said Marco.

"Even better," said Derek. "See you then."

He closed the phone.

"I thought you were going to make an appointment for *me*," said Candice.

Derek gestured to the basement stairs. "This is better."

"Better how?"

He moved forward, herding her in front of him. "Marco knows me. He trusts me."

She reluctantly started down the first couple of steps. "But your schedule."

"Like I said, you caught me on a quiet day."

"I can do this myself," she grumbled.

"I know you can." Derek typed in another quick message to his secretary as he followed Candy into the basement.

THEY SEARCHED THE REST of the basement but didn't find anything else that excited Candy. So Derek gathered up the stack of guest registers and the old menus and loaded them into his car.

He drove Candy to the Sea Shanty. There, he found Marco had snagged a table near the rail of the covered sundeck, overlooking the beach.

The weather was unseasonably warm. The wind was calm and the tide was low. Couples and families wandered the sand, collecting shells, making castles and soaking up the last warm rays before the cool, fall weather moved in. A child's occasional shout mixed with the background murmurs of the other Sea Shanty patrons.

"We're researching the history of the Quayside Hotel," said Derek after the cocktail waitress had taken their margarita order.

"How far back you planning to go?" asked Marco.

Candy jumped in, expression alight. "I found the original guest registers in the basement. I'm hoping there might be a famous person or two on the list."

Marco smiled brightly at Candy, giving Derek a brief shot of jealousy. He shook it away.

"Like the time Prince Ivan and Princess Katrina stayed in the Roosevelt suite?"

Candy straightened. "They did?"

Marco's forehead furrowed. "Midforties, if my grandfather's stories are accurate."

Candy leaned forward, propping her elbow on the smooth birch table. "What happened?"

Marco shifted his cushioned chair closer and leaned in toward her, drinking up her smile and the sound of her voice. "I believe they ordered the pheasant from room service."

Candy's shoulders slumped. "That's it?"

Derek didn't know whether to be sorry she didn't get the story she was looking for, or pleased that Marco had disappointed her. When he planned this little get-together, he hadn't considered they might be attracted to each other. And he sure hadn't considered that he might care.

"Well, they took over the whole floor with their attendants and security staff."

"No interesting stories?" asked Candy.

"Is that what you want?" asked Marco in a smooth, honeyed tone that set Derek's teeth on edge.

"Yes," said Candy.

"Then we should talk about David Stone and Jake Seymour."

"The club singers?"

"The bad boys," said Marco with a nod and a twinkle, his hand inching its way across the table.

Derek cleared his throat. "We're planning on using these stories for the Historical Society."

Marco seemed to suddenly remember Derek was there. "Oh." He winked at Candy. "Better save that one for another time."

Derek was really starting to rethink the plan of using Marco for information. It wasn't like he could tell Marco to back off. It was none of his damn business if Marco came on to Candy, or if Candy encouraged it.

The waitress arrived with their margaritas, and Derek took a long drink of the tart lime and golden tequila.

"Got anything interesting, yet G-rated?" asked Candy.

"There was the time Adele Albingnon checked in with her seven Pekingese."

Candy stirred her icy drink and nodded. "Now we're talking."

"We had a 'no pets' policy at the time. But when a dog shows up with a collar worth more than your car, you rethink the policy."

The noise level on the deck started to rise as the after-work crowd grew, and Candy leaned closer to Marco, hanging on his every word.

"Each dog had a little plaid coat, a bow in its hair and its very own nanny," said Marco.

Candy laughed.

"They ordered sautéed liver and ground filet mignon, and had it delivered on silver platters. Of course, my grandfather made sure the dishes were never used for people again."

"Any chance they're still around?" asked Candy.

"The dishes?"

No, the dogs. Derek took a swig of his slush drink.

Candy nodded at Marco.

He shrugged. "I don't know how we'd find them. Though we might have some photographs back at the house. Maybe you could get some reproductions."

Candy sat back, her eyes went wide, and she blinked in astonishment. "You've got pictures?"

"Some old albums from Grandpa's attic. You want to stop by the house and pick them up?"

Candy's tone turned reverent. "Could I?"

"I'll get them tomorrow," Derek quickly put in.

They both turned to look at him.

"It's on my way," he said to Candy.

She opened her mouth, and Derek just knew she was going to make this difficult. But Marco beat her to it. With a very calculating look in his eye, he gave Derek a two-fingered salute. "Sure thing, Derek."

Oh, great. Now Marco had the wrong idea.

10

"I'VE GOT THE ALBUMS," assured Derek's smooth, sexy voice over the telephone line.

Candice squelched her physical reaction as she gave Jenna a thumbs-up signal across the reception area of the Canna Interiors offices. "Don't you dare open them," she said to Derek.

He laughed. "Wouldn't dream of doing it without you. Can you do lunch?"

Candice fought a shiver. "Lunch? Sure. Jenna wants to come, too."

"She does?" asked Derek.

Jenna shook her head, making a slashing motion across her throat.

Candice nodded insistently at Jenna. Jenna it's-like-a-chocolate-craving Reeves *owed* her on this.

It had been less than seventy-two hours since she'd made love to Derek, and the craving was back to full strength. And after her second margarita last night, he'd started looking unimaginably sexy. She didn't trust herself alone with him.

"I can't," Jenna whispered.

Candice covered the mouthpiece of the phone. "Yes, you can."

"Probably the easiest thing to do is meet at my place," said Derek.

"*Your* place?" Candice squeaked into the phone.

"Yeah. I left the registers and the menus there last night."

Candice cursed under her breath. She knew she should have taken the treasures home with her. But she'd called a taxi and escaped from the Sea Shanty while Derek and Marco were engrossed in a conversation about overseas markets. She'd been afraid of what might happen if Derek drove her home.

Jenna grinned at her. "*His* place?"

Candice covered the receiver. "You are *so* coming with me."

"I'm meeting Tyler."

"Tough."

"Candy?"

"Yes, Derek?"

"Want me to pick you up?"

"No. That's okay. *We'll* meet you there."

Jenna shook her head.

Candice nodded at her again.

"Sounds good," said Derek. "See you then."

"Goodbye." She hung up the phone.

"Not coming," sang Jenna.

"Canceling on your husband," said Candice.

"It's our four-month anniversary."

"Celebrate tonight."

"He'll be here in five minutes."

"Then we'd better hurry."

Jenna took a couple of backward steps into the doorway of her office. "This lust for Derek is *your* problem."

Candice advanced on her. "You're the one who told me to sleep with him."

"You're the one who liked it."

"I didn't… Okay, so I did."

"Do it again. Can't hurt. Might help."

"You think I'm taking your advice a second time?"

Jenna just grinned.

The outer door to the reception area opened, and Tyler stuck his head in. "Ready, babe?"

"Ready," Jenna called to her husband.

Candice slumped in defeat. "I'm a chocoholic," she whispered for Jenna's ears only.

Jenna paused to pat her on the shoulder. "We'll get you into a twelve-step program."

CANDICE WAS PRETTY SURE this was a bad bet for step one of her program. She parked her car in Derek's driveway and set the brake, staring at his front door while she screwed up her courage.

She had no choice. He had the menus. He had the registers. And he had the photo albums.

Worse, Myrna West had called this morning. It seemed the Historical Society required the property owner—Derek—to make the formal presentation on Saturday. Candice needed him more than ever.

She gathered her stack of library books and two file folders from the passenger seat of her MG and wrenched the door open. Short juniper bushes lined the curving, exposed aggregate pathway to Derek's wide front porch. She could see the lake behind his big house and guessed he had a million-dollar view from the top floor.

He probably had a European art collection and custom-made furniture. That was good. It would remind her he was one of them—a cold-hearted, mercenary man who could spit out hearts like sunflower husks. Maybe he wouldn't look so attractive next to a million-dollar Menzuzzi painting.

She rang the bell.

A plump, gray-haired woman immediately opened the door and greeted her with a smile.

A housekeeper? Derek had a housekeeper?

Saved by his high-living ways, she smiled broadly at the woman. "Candice Hammond. Derek is expecting me."

"Candice." Derek strode down the polished hardwood of his long hallway.

The housekeeper gestured to the library books. "Can I help you with those?"

"I've got them, Mrs. Bartel," said Derek, lifting the books from Candice's hands. "Thanks."

He nodded back down the hallway. "Thought we'd meet in the sunroom."

Candice thanked Mrs. Bartel and followed Derek down the hall. The sunroom. That didn't sound too intimate. It sounded like the place with lots of windows, bright light, a housekeeper wandering in and out all lunch hour long. She'd worried for nothing.

Derek pushed open a curtained French door and held it for her. Candice stepped through the doorway, and then stopped short. This wasn't a sunroom, it was a full-fledged tropical garden. Stone pillars lined a flagstone path. They were surrounded by leafy potted plants and covered with woody vines.

The path led to a rock garden around a goldfish pond with a trickling waterfall. Comfortable groupings of polished wicker furniture and towering fifteen-foot palm trees were placed at intervals.

Candice turned in a circle, looking all around. "This is stunning."

Derek smiled. "You should see it at night. The landscaper put pot lights in the fountain, and you can see the stars through the glass ceiling."

He set the library books down on a glass table. The menus and hotel registers were already there, along with what had to be the photo albums from Marco.

"I'd love to see it at night," she breathed, before she realized what she was saying.

"Anytime," said Derek, gesturing to one of the ivory cushioned seats.

He sat down with her and opened the top file folder. "What've you got here?"

"You don't need to worry about that," said Candice. "What is it?"

"The application form. I've rounded up some of the chronology of the building and jotted down the significant milestones. Now we need to add the amusing anecdotes." She picked up the first of the photo albums. "Think Marco would help us out again?"

Derek looked up from reading the application form. "Why?"

Candice didn't understand the question. "So he can tell us more stories...."

"I'll talk to him," said Derek with a frown.

She didn't understand why Derek would want to waste his time? "But—"

"Don't worry," he cut in. "I'll take good notes."

"I don't want you to go to any trouble."

Derek went back to reading. "No trouble."

Something was strange here. "Derek?"

"Hmm?"

"I know you're a busy man."

"I'll take care of Marco." He closed the folder. "So, what's the game plan?"

It was on the tip of Candice's tongue to argue some more. But she didn't want to annoy him.

If Derek was hell-bent on talking to Marco, fine with her. As long as she got the stories she needed. "I'm going to check out the pictures. If I recognize some of the people who stayed at the hotel in the forties, I'll talk to Marco and see if I can build the presentation around them."

"You mean, *I'll* talk to Marco."

She placed an album on the glass table between them and opened it up. "Fine."

Derek scooted his chair a little closer.

The pictures were old, mostly blurry black and white, stuck into the album by black paper corners. They were captioned in white ink, and pages crackled as she turned them.

Even blurry, it was a treasure trove.

Candice gasped and exclaimed and speculated on person after person, until Derek finally picked up the phone and put Marco on speaker to answer her questions.

She scribbled notes for nearly an hour, laughing and marveling at the stories Marco told her as her confidence in the presentation grew. Then Marco had to leave for a meeting, so Derek hung up the phone.

"You like Marco, don't you?" he asked.

"He's currently my hero," said Candice, flipping through the pages of notes. "These are fantastic. But I don't know how we'll use them all."

"He's got a reputation as a womanizer, you know."

Candice looked up. "Huh? You mean Martin Spain?" Martin Spain was an industrialist who stayed at the hotel during the sixties. He brought along an endless parade of starlets, models and debutantes.

"I mean Marco," said Derek, looking annoyed.

"I wasn't planning to write about Marco." Candice realized they couldn't present any of the stories of sex and debauchery to the Historical Society. Myrna West and her blue-haired friends would probably faint dead away.

"I meant for you," said Derek, voice gruff.

She turned to stare at him. Things had been going so well. She'd almost forgotten about his unpredictable temper.

"Have I stayed too long?" she asked. Maybe she'd made him late for a meeting.

She started to stand, gathering up the scattered books and papers. "I can get out of your—"

Derek stood with her. "We haven't even had lunch yet."

"But if you're late…"

"I'm not late."

She paused. "Then what's wrong?"

Derek crossed his arms, looking huge and imposing. "I don't want you getting mixed up with Marco."

Candice blinked. Now she was really confused. "But you introduced us…."

Derek looked away. "I know. But he's no good for you."

Candice moved her head so she was looking Derek in the eye again. "I'm using his stories, not dating him."

Derek pinned her with a piercing gaze.

Comprehension dawned. "Ohhh. You think I'm interested…"

"Aren't you?"

Candice fought a grin, shaking her head. "Not in the least." Marco was a nice guy and all. But he was a little like an untrained puppy, all bounding energy and scattered enthusiasm. The kind of guy who went through women like rubber chew toys.

"You sure?" asked Derek.

Oh, yeah. Candice was sure. She'd met dozens of Marcos in her time. Derek didn't need to warn her off.

She crossed her arms, imitating his pose. "I'm working on a business presentation, Derek. Sex is the furthest thing from my mind."

Now there was a lie. As she stared at Derek's stern face, her skin started to get that familiar itchy feeling. The sound of the waterfall rose in her ears, and she realized that sex with Derek was exactly what was on her mind.

Derek's eyes darkened as the moment drew out. "Funny," he said. "Sex has been on my mind constantly since—"

Panic shot from Candice's toes to her chest. "Don't."

He dropped his arms to his sides. He didn't move, but he suddenly seemed closer. "Don't what?"

Her heart rate spiked. "We can't do it again, Derek."

"Why not?"

"Because this is business. You're working with my father. I'm your sister-in-law's business partner. We've already made it complicated enough." And, like Marco, he would chew her up and spit her out when he was done.

"You think making love a second time is going to make any difference at all?"

Yes!

But she was tempted. Oh, how badly she was tempted.

"And then what, Derek?" she forced herself to say. "A third time? A fourth? A fifth? Where do we stop? We can handle it now." At least she thought she could handle it now. She didn't dare entertain the idea that she was past the point of no return.

"You're gorgeous," he said.

"You're incorrigible." She knew resistance was her only option. She couldn't imagine any twelve-step program that involved indulging in the addiction.

"It's part of my charm," he said. "Makes women want to tear off their clothes."

Candice glanced down at the rough flagstone floor and shivered at the thought of the chill on her bare skin. "Here? With your housekeeper waiting in the wings? I don't think so, Derek."

"I've got a bedroom."

"I bet you do."

"Door locks."

She stiffened her spine. "I've got work to do. You want to help, or should I find someplace quiet to concentrate?"

"There's not a hope in hell you'll say yes, is there?"

Candice shook her head.

"Then I'll help with the presentation."

There it was. Her opening to say she needed him

to deliver the presentation on Saturday. It wasn't exactly the perfect time to ask a favor, but the clock was ticking.

"Glad you're willing to help." She forced a cheerful note into her voice. "Because the Society wants you to make the formal presentation on Saturday."

Derek's eyebrows went up. "Me?"

She nodded. "Their policy is to only receive requests from the owner."

A smile grew on Derek's face and a calculating twinkle rose in his eyes. She knew that expression. He wanted to get a negotiation going.

She took a step back. "Not a chance."

"I didn't ask for anything."

"You're about to."

He inched closer. "Can we get a negotiation going here or not?"

"I'm not having sex with you in exchange for the presentation."

"Who said anything about sex?"

"I'm not stupid. You've been talking about sex for the past ten minutes."

"I've been thinking about sex for the past four weeks."

Candice stood her ground. "You agreed the heritage designation would boost community goodwill, and you could use it as a media campaign springboard. *I'm* the one doing *you* a favor. You should give me something in return."

His grin widened. "Anytime, anyplace."

Candice groaned.

"I was going to ask you for a kiss, Candy."

"A kiss?"

"A kiss."

Her eyes narrowed. "You remember what happened last time we bargained for kisses."

"Definitely."

"This is not a good idea."

"As you so correctly pointed out, Mrs. Bartel is likely to walk in anytime. She may know most of my secrets, but I don't think she'd appreciate witnessing my sex life first hand."

Candice sifted through the possibilities in her mind. She could handle a kiss, particularly if it secured his participation on Saturday.

"Only a kiss?" she asked.

"Right."

"Won't lead anywhere else?"

He nodded.

"I kiss you, and you make the presentation."

"Absolutely."

"Saturday. Ten o'clock."

"I'll be there."

"For one kiss?"

"Two."

Candice took a bracing breath and fastened the top buttons on her blouse. Sometimes a woman had to do what a woman had to do.

Derek chuckled. "Want to slip into a chastity belt?"

"Probably a good idea."

"You know we've been talking about kissing for longer than it'll take to do it?"

Candice smiled. "I need to make sure the deal is ironclad."

Derek moved forward, gently taking her hand and drawing her to him. "You want to come and work for me someday?"

"Doing what?"

"Labor negotiations. You're dynamite."

"Only because you're weak and you don't date often enough."

"You think I'm so attracted to you because I haven't been with a woman in a while."

"Seems like a safe bet."

He touched his index finger to the bottom of her chin. "You'd lose, Candy."

She sucked in a tight breath as a hum of sensation started with his fingertips and cascaded through her body. Her hands went limp, and the pen she'd been holding dropped onto the table. The *whoosh* of the waterfall filled her ears.

Desire for Derek overloaded her senses, and she subconsciously leaned toward him.

"I'm taking this as a yes," he whispered as his palm cupped her chin and his other arm went around her.

"Yes," she whispered in return, pressing against his chest, wrapping her arms around his big body. He was strong and as solid and hard as granite.

His hot lips pressed against hers, gentle, firmer, harder. It was territory they both knew well and neither hesitated to open their mouths and deepen the kiss.

It was good. It was better than anything Candice had felt in her life. It might only be a kiss, but it filled her entire body with liquid warmth. Her extremities tingled. Her skin warmed. Her senses sharpened as the essence of Derek surrounded and flooded her.

One kiss turned to two, and then three, and then four. She wanted more. She wanted skin on skin.

They could do it. It could be quick. It could be lightning if Derek felt half the desperation she did.

On the love seat? Behind the fountain? Beneath the leaves of a lush bush?

The door at the end of the pillared pathway opened with a clatter.

Derek drew back, setting Candice away from him.

He glanced at his watch. "Right on time," he breathed.

Candice blinked, gasping, struggling to get her bearings. "You knew when she was coming?"

He gently lowered Candice into her chair. "A smart man compensates for his own weaknesses."

11

SMART MIGHT BE A BIT of a stretch, but Derek was definitely weak when it came to Candy. For the next three days, he forced himself to stay away from her. Though she'd acknowledged the chemistry between them, she insisted she didn't want anything physical.

Unfortunately, Derek desperately wanted something physical. And he was a very goal-oriented guy. He knew the only way to stop himself from trying to change her mind was to keep his distance.

So they'd talked on the phone and faxed drafts of the presentation back and forth. He found himself spending an inordinate amount of time on her project, rearranging his schedule to accommodate her phone calls, then working late every night to compensate.

The schedule was grueling, even for him.

Late Friday afternoon, his brothers called him on it. They convinced him to join in on the last beach barbecue of the season. He'd agreed and showed up at Pacific Beach. But with Candy wreaking havoc on his time-management skills, he was contemplating how early he could cut out and get back to the balance sheet for the Electronics Division.

He moved to where Jenna was setting dishes on the picnic table, the red plastic tablecloth billowing in the breeze. "I'm sorry, Jenna, but I'm going to have to—"

He did a double take as a silver MG pulled into the parking lot above the concrete retaining wall.

Candy?

He squinted through the windshield of the car as the female driver shifted it into park and set the brake. She reached for something on the seat beside her, and he saw her profile.

It *was* Candy.

"You have to what?" Jenna prompted, passing him a stack of glasses.

"Nothing." He shook his head, automatically putting the glasses at the place settings in front of him. "Never mind."

It would be rude to take off as soon as Candy arrived. And he could handle seeing her on a public beach. It wasn't like there'd be an opportunity to proposition her.

She pushed open the driver's door and stepped out, wearing cream-colored jeans and a mauve raw-silk blouse. The sleeves were long, but the ties at the neck were loose, and the filmy fabric drooped casually over her smooth, golden shoulders. She waved, giving Jenna a wide smile, but her expression faltered when her gaze landed on Derek.

Derek raised his eyebrows at Jenna. "You didn't tell Candy I was going to be here, did you?"

Jenna smirked. *"Candy?"*

"Candice," Derek quickly corrected, wondering how much his family had gossiped about them.

"You think she needed a warning?"

"Of course not," Derek lied. "We're friends."

"Just *friends?*" asked Jenna.

"She doesn't want anything more," Derek admitted.

"That's because she's scared of you."

He breathed out a laugh. That was ridiculous. "Candy's not scared of anything. She's tough as nails."

She'd beat the crap out of him over the carpet, the leather upholstery and everything else they'd ever disagreed on. She'd had him jumping to attention all week long. She even had him blocking off his entire Saturday morning to talk to little old ladies about the esthetic value of historic bricks.

And, sexually speaking, she had him wrapped around her little finger. He should be the one scared of her.

Around the corner of her trunk lid, he could see her struggling to lift a big red cooler.

"Be right back," he said to Jenna, leaving the glasses to take the concrete stairs two at a time.

"Need help?" He lifted the cooler out of Candy's hands without waiting for her answer.

She met his gaze dead on. "Hey, Derek."

Didn't seem scared of him so far. "How's it

going?" he asked, watching her closely, just in case Jenna was right.

She pushed the trunk shut and shrugged her beach bag onto her shoulder. "I'm fine. You?"

So much for Candy quaking in her boots. They were friends. Friends with a chemistry thing.

"I'm great." He turned toward the staircase that led back to the beach. He *was* great. He suddenly felt lighter, more relaxed than he had in days.

"Read the final draft this afternoon," he said as he started down the stairs. "Looks like we're ready to rock and roll."

She fell into step beside him. "I scanned the rest of the pictures in for the computer presentation. Finished about an hour ago."

They hit the sand. "Should we meet early tomorrow to rehearse?"

Candice bent to strip off her sandals. "You think we should?"

Derek paused to wait for her. "A dry run is always a good idea. My office?"

"Sure."

He smiled at her, feeling better by the minute. He held up the cooler. "I'll put this in the shade."

"Thanks."

"No problem."

Jenna and Erin joined Candice as Derek headed for a shady spot where the retaining wall curved back on itself.

Tyler and Striker sauntered over, eyeing up

Candy's cooler in Derek's arms, both grinning knowingly.

Derek clamped his jaw, set down the cooler then straightened. "Just because *you* two don't have the manners God gave a hound, doesn't mean I can't act like a gentleman."

Their grins widened.

"Toast," muttered Tyler.

"Crispy," said Striker.

Derek scowled.

"Volleyball?" called Jenna.

"You bet," said Derek, feeling a sudden need for physical activity.

They gathered at a beach volleyball net fifty feet from their picnic site. First Erin and Striker beat Jenna and Tyler. Then Candy and Derek beat the other teams in two straight games to claim the championship.

Despite her willowy model shape, Candy turned out to be a darn good player. Her athleticism surprised Derek, though her competitive spirit was no less than he'd expected. Jenna was nuts. Candy knew no fear.

While the barbecue warmed up and the sun dipped toward the Pacific, the women sipped fruity cocktails on the beach blankets while Derek joined his brothers for Frisbee.

Whenever Tyler made a good catch, Jenna would cheer. And Erin called out when Striker was successful.

Derek tried not to mind the silence after his moves.

But when he made a particularly stunning dive catch that sent him rolling across the sand with the white Frisbee clutched tightly against his chest, he couldn't help but look up at Candy.

She grinned at him, giving a thumbs-up.

He felt like he'd just caught a touchdown pass at the Super Bowl. He jumped to his feet, a silly, self-satisfied grin on his face as he tossed the Frisbee back to Striker.

By the time they finished Frisbee and devoured the hamburgers, it was dark enough to light a fire. As the air temperature dropped and the other beach-goers headed home, they arranged the blankets around the orange flickering bonfire.

Small waves lapped on the sand twenty feet away, burbling instead of roaring now that the tide had reached high slack. The night was clear and the stars as bright as diamonds.

Jenna cuddled up to Tyler, and Erin leaned back against Striker's chest. The conversation took a lull as the two couples exchanged quick whispers.

Derek's arms suddenly felt empty.

He wished he could join Candy on the other side of the fire. She'd fit so nicely between his legs, warm and soft against his chest. He'd wrap his arms around her, rub the goose bumps from her shoulders, inhale the fresh scent of her hair, feel her body hum as she spoke to him in low tones.

He'd love to hold her in his arms. But it was out of the question. Their relationship was too...

Relationship?

He pulled that thought up short.

His glance flicked to her face.

She looked out of place and uncomfortable, sitting between the two loving couples. Kind of like how he felt.

He stood. "Walk on the beach, Candice?"

Gratitude flashed across her face. "Sure."

The other four barely seemed to notice when they left the circle of the firelight. Derek took up Candy's hand. She didn't pull away, and he felt his body relax.

"Nice catch," she said.

He smiled. "Thanks. You've got one hell of a volleyball serve."

She laughed, swinging their joined hands in wide arcs. "And you're a handsome man, with impeccable taste and good manners."

"Thank God no one is listening to us."

"It could be a little embarrassing."

Derek didn't feel embarrassed. He felt silly and giddy and happy. He wished the beach would stretch out forever, so they could keep walking and walking. Maybe if they talked long enough, he'd figure out what was going on between them.

He thought about what Jenna had told him and sobered. "Candy?"

She obviously sensed the change in his mood. She stopped swinging their arms. "Yeah?"

"Jenna said something earlier…"

Candy stiffened.

Maybe it was true. "She told me—"

"Derek."

"—that you were scared of me."

Candy stopped in her tracks. "Scared?"

He turned to face her. Cool light from the rising moon outlined her face. She wasn't wearing makeup, still her skin was flawlessly smooth, her lashes long and dark, and her lips the color of roses. She was definitely the most beautiful woman in the world.

His voice dropped to a whisper. "I don't want you to be scared of me, Candy."

She gave him a half smile and shook her head. "I'm not scared—"

"Good."

"—exactly."

"What do you mean, *exactly?*"

"You put me off balance," she admitted.

He took her other hand and braced his feet on the soft sand. He was about as off balance as a guy could get. "Because I turn you on?" he asked, hopefully.

"Because I never know what you're thinking," she neatly sidestepped.

"Want to know what I'm thinking now?"

"I'm not sure."

"I'm thinking you're gorgeous."

"Derek."

"I'm thinking I want to kiss you."

"Don't say—"

"But then, I'm always thinking I want to kiss you."

He didn't wait for her to react to that, just leaned forward and put his desires into action.

She didn't pull away, she softened.

He slipped his arms around her waist, and hers wound around his neck. The kiss was slow and gentle, long and satisfying. This is what he'd wanted back at the fire. Candy, him, touching, together.

He needed to hold her tight and keep the world away. Just for a little while. Just until he felt centered. Just until he could breathe without wanting her.

He kissed her cheek, her temple, her ear, inhaling her scent, reveling in the touch of her silky smooth skin.

She moaned his name and pressed against him, a beacon drawing him closer, pulling him toward something he didn't understand. All he knew was that it mattered. She mattered.

"Come home with me," he whispered.

"But—"

"I need you, Candy." The words sounded raw. They felt raw. His chest was burning and his limbs were starting to tremble.

She glanced back at the glowing dot of the bonfire in the distance. "They'll wonder what—"

"I don't care."

"We can't just—"

"Yes, we can." He touched her chin, tilting her face up toward him, pulling back just enough to gaze into her gold-green eyes. "We can…"

He took a deep breath, holding it, stepping dangerously far out onto a limb. "Do you want to come home with me, Candy?"

The wind stood still.

The waves seemed to stop.

She stared, unblinking while his world paused.

Then her lashes fluttered down and her hands convulsed against the back of his neck. "Yes."

HE NEEDED HER.

Candice didn't know about other women, but apparently those words floated her boat. On the ride from the beach to Derek's house, it was all she could do not to beg him to pull over so she could jump him right there in the cramped front seat of the Porsche.

She'd restrained herself, but barely.

He parked the car haphazardly, and they raced up his front stairs. He closed the door behind them. The house was dark except for the glow of the yard lights coming through the big windows.

Without a word, he took her hand and led her toward the stairs.

"Housekeeper?" she asked.

"Not tonight." He strode for the top landing.

His long legs let him take the stairs two at a time, and she struggled to keep up.

He pushed open the door to a magnificent master bedroom.

The blinds were up, and the lights from the yard filtered in through the paned windows. The ceiling was high A block-patterned moss-green-and-gold quilt covered a king-sized, four-poster bed. And champagne armchairs framed a set of French doors that obviously led to a balcony.

"Lights?" he asked.

She shook her head.

"Wine?" he asked.

Her chest tightened, and she took her courage in both hands, shaking her head again. "Just you. Now."

He pulled her into his arms, nuzzling her neck, planting small kisses that made her shiver. "Oh, Candy. If you knew how many times…I've pictured you right here."

His words warmed her. Her nerves settled. Jenna was right. She wasn't seventeen anymore.

"Pictured me doing what?" she boldly asked.

He chuckled low. "I don't think you want me to tell you that."

She cocked her head, pulling back to look him in the eyes. She gave him a mischievous smiled. "Yeah. I do."

His eyes darkened with passion as he drew in a shuddering breath.

She wriggled her blouse over her head and stood in front of him in her wispy bra. "'Cause, if you don't tell me, how am I going to know what to do?"

"Candy."

"In *my* bedroom," she continued. "I always pictured you naked."

"You pictured me in your bedroom?"

She nodded meaningfully to his clothes. "Naked."

"Not a problem." He stripped off his T-shirt and

stepped out of his shorts, standing there big and bronze and beautiful.

In the back of the limo, she hadn't had a chance to look her fill. Now she did. He was spectacular, from the tip of his toes to his thick, dark hair and every inch in between.

"Better than my imagination," she said.

With a grunt of satisfaction, he reached forward and tucked his fingers into the front waistband of her low-cut jeans, tugging her toward him. "I always pictured you in silk and satin."

"Got anything around here I should slip into?"

He popped the button on the top of her jeans. "Nope." Then he slowly slid down the zipper. "You got anything good under here?"

"You tell me."

He brushed his knuckles across the front of her silk panties. "Oh, yeah."

Sensation shot through her, and she braced her hands on his shoulders.

He pushed her jeans out of the way, and she leaned into his chest, kissing his pecs, tasting his salty skin, memorizing the feel and scent of his body.

"You were on my bed," he muttered against her hair. "Naked. Smiling. And I knew... I just knew..." He pulled back to look into her eyes.

Candice snapped the clasp on her bra and let it drop to the floor. Then she shimmied out of her panties. She felt totally uninhibited in her nakedness—sexy, not at all self-conscious.

Derek's eyes turned slumberous, turning her on. She wanted this *so* bad.

She took a backward step toward the bed, stretching out her arm to hold Derek's hand, encouraging him to come along with her.

He moved easily toward her.

When the backs of her legs met the cool, smooth comforter, she sat down. "Like this?"

"Lie back," he rasped.

She did, laying her head back on the silky throw pillows.

He dropped to his knees on the floor beside her. "You're perfect." His tone was reverent. He trailed a fingertip along the curve of her waist, over her hip bone, skimming the top of her thigh.

Then he smiled. "Think I'll just sit here and watch you all night long."

Candice turned her head and raised her eyebrows. "Not much fun in that for me."

"You want more?" he asked with mock amazement.

"Much more."

"Yeah? How're you going to convince me?"

She sat up, turning, dangling her legs over the edge of the bed, his face level with her breasts. "Is this a negotiation, Derek Reeves?"

His gaze fixated on her breasts. "Everything between us is a negotiation." He leaned forward and kissed one of her nipples.

She moaned, tipping her head back, sliding closer to him.

"Trouble is," he said, kissing the other nipple, then pushing her back and slipping up between her legs until they were face to face. "You're way better at it than I am. Crook your little finger, and I'm yours for life."

The slide of his body teased her tender skin. His sweet breath fanned her face. She inhaled, lifting her head, stretching to taste his mouth.

He met her halfway, his body weight pinning her against the mattress, his mouth hot and hungry and confident. Sensation zipped through every corner of her body. She wrapped her arms around his broad back, kissing, suckling, holding him tighter and tighter.

There was no way to get close enough.

She bent her knees, bringing her heels up onto the bed.

"Candy," he rasped.

"Now," she moaned.

"But—"

She arched her back, spreading her arms wide on the bed. "My breasts for your—"

He swore between clenched teeth. He was inside her before she could blink.

Finally.

Close enough.

She wrapped herself around him, holding on tight while he kissed her, caressed her and thrust himself inside her over and over and over again.

She wanted it to last forever, needed it to last forever, but too soon everything blurred in front of her eyes and Derek's breathing rasped in her ears. The sweat was slick between them, and passion rose to nearly painful heights before he cried out her name and the world imploded.

Aftershocks tingled through her body as she labored to catch her breath. Derek was heavy on top of her, but she held on, not wanting him to move. It was like floating in heaven. Every cell in her body was limp with satisfaction, and a mind-numbing glow warmed her soul.

"Nobody does that to me," she whispered in awe.

"Nobody does that to anybody," Derek whispered back. "I think we discovered a new plane of existence."

Candice nodded in agreement as the room came back into focus. Derek's room. Where he'd pictured her.

All those nights, while she was fantasizing about him, he was fantasizing about her.

Amazing.

"So, did I get it right?" she asked, half joking.

His voice was serious, even reverent. "You got it so damn right." Then he rolled onto his back, like he'd done in the limo, taking her with him, keeping them entwined, while taking his weight off her.

He flipped the comforter over her back, smoothing it down, pushing her hair back from her forehead and stroking his palm down its length. "I have laid here so many nights thinking about you."

Candice's chest expanded with joy until it was so tight it hurt. She had to ask. "How many?"

"Afraid I lost count."

"When did it start?"

"It started with that silly kiss in the Tunnel of Love. When I found out who you were. When I realized just how complicated our relationship was going to get."

She pulled back a couple of inches. "You've been hot for me all this time? Heck, I've only been fantasizing about you since—"

"You always have to win, don't you?"

She paused. Okay, so he deserved her honesty. "I've been hot for you since the first time you lied to me. Guess you win this round."

He kissed her sweet mouth. "I think we both win this round. You want to check out my hot tub?"

She took a deep breath and nodded. "Oh, yeah."

LATER, CANDICE LAY in Derek's arms, spoon fashion, with him behind her, staring through the open French doors to the lights of Seattle across the lake.

"Did I ever say thank you?" she asked.

He chuckled. "No need to thank me. It was my pleasure."

She dug her elbow into his ribs. "For helping me with the Lighthouse designation."

"Oh, that."

"Yeah. That." She relaxed again, picturing the finished restaurant in her mind. "It's always been my dream, you know."

"A heritage restaurant?"

"Heritage buildings. Honoring our history by preserving the past. You can't quantify it in dollars and cents, but it makes sense deep down." She stopped. "I guess you don't understand that, do you?"

"Explain it to me."

"I've always thought there were things in life more important than money."

"And you call yourself a Hammond?"

She elbowed him again, more gently this time. "You'd make a better Hammond than me. I was always the black sheep, the artistic one, the impractical one."

"I thought you got along great with your family. What with the ongoing discussions of semen and all."

Candice smiled. "Oh, they like me well enough. They just don't understand me."

His arms tightened around her. "That's because you're a complicated woman."

"You don't understand me, either, do you?"

"Not completely."

"You can't understand giving up money for beauty."

His voice inched toward his debating tone. "I'm all for beauty. But there are some practical realities that have to be met before we have the luxury of focusing on art."

"Such as?"

"Food, shelter, clothing…"

"Most people in Seattle have food, shelter and clothing," Candice countered. "What they're missing is art, heritage and culture. That's the food for your soul."

"Your soul can't survive without a body."

"And there's no point in having a body survive without your soul."

A moment passed in silence. "You think I have a soul, Candy?"

The question startled her. "Of course you have a soul." Sure, he was a hard-ass businessman, compelled to make money every single day of his life. But he was also a gentle and generous lover. And watching him goof off with his brothers tonight had shown her a touchingly human side.

"Maybe just smaller than most," he joked.

Candice didn't know how to answer that. She was beginning to suspect he had a seriously soft heart under that tough exterior.

She was starting to hope she'd been wrong about him, starting to hope for something more than a quick fling. But that was a dangerous line of thinking. She needed to take this for what it was, not set herself up for heartache.

"Maybe just smaller than most," she agreed.

They fell silent, as an evergreen-scented wind wafted through the window and traffic hummed softly on the faraway interstate. Derek's breathing gradually evened out and his arms relaxed.

Wide-awake, Candice gazed out over the city, telling herself their interlude was almost over. It was nearly two in the morning, and they had to make the presentation later that day at ten. After that, there was no reason for them to be together, no reason to continue their relationship.

She gritted her teeth, reminding herself she'd gone into this with her eyes wide-open. She tensed, preparing to drag herself out of his warm bed and get on with the rest of her life.

But before she could move, his hand tightened on her stomach. He wasn't asleep, and his voice was a rough whisper in her ear. "Stay."

She froze. *Stay?*

His words were strained, his muscles taut. "Just…" A full minute ticked by. "Stay."

One word. A single word. But it shifted the foundation of her life.

She'd tried so hard to keep him out of her heart, but he was in solid, and there was nothing she could do to help herself. She felt a stray tear burn the back of her eyelid. "Okay."

He rolled her onto her back, kissing her gently on the lips.

She kissed him back, holding him close, trying to sort out the chaos inside her. He was going to hold her all night long. They were going to wake up together in the same bed.

Where were they going? What were they doing?

He broke the kiss and pulled back.

She stared into his dark eyes, searching for answers she knew he didn't have. "Derek?"

He shook his head. "I don't know, Candy."

She touched his face, rough beneath her fingertips, nearly time for him to shave again.

He kissed her gently one more time, and she wrapped her arms around him, pulling him tight, trying to absorb his essence and quell her fears. If this went wrong, she was going to get hurt so badly.

12

DEREK STOOD AT THE HEAD of the table in the small Historical Society boardroom in front of Myrna West and the five other board members, trying to keep his mind on the presentation and off of Candy. He hit a key on his laptop computer, bringing up the next historical photograph, launching into the story of Adele Albingnon and her seven Pekingese.

But his gaze strayed to Candy, and he catapulted into the depths of her emerald eyes, in danger of getting aroused right here at the front of the room. The minute this was over, they were heading back to his place. He'd blow off his afternoon appointments and spend the rest of the day with Candy.

Definitely.

But that was later. Right now he had to get through the presentation without embarrassing himself.

He quickly switched his attention to Myrna, then to William Swinney and Miriam Jones.

That fixed it.

He finished the Pekingese story, then turned up the lights. He passed around copies of the original architectural drawings and explained how the Canna Interiors renovation had restored features of the original building.

"Excellent presentation," said Myrna, beaming at her fellow board members.

They all smiled and nodded in agreement.

Derek dared a glance at Candy. Her face was flushed, her smile wide and her jewel eyes sparkled with joy. Apparently this was almost as good as sex.

Myrna opened a folder and retrieved a multi-page agreement. "There will have to be a final vote at our monthly meeting, of course." She handed the agreement to Derek. "But I think I can guarantee the vote will be favorable. If you could sign pages six and eleven, I'll have the board secretary send you an official copy after the vote."

Derek took the agreement, flipping through the pages, considering whether he should have the legal department take a quick look at it before he signed. A clause on page seven jumped out at him.

That couldn't be right.

He looked up at Myrna. "The board can veto a future sale?"

She nodded. "I'm sure you can understand how the board will need a measure of control over the designated site."

"But we're not going to sell the restaurant. It's part

of the hotel. We could lease it, maybe. But we couldn't sell it on its own."

William Swinney spoke up. "But you *could* sell the hotel."

Derek stared at the man for a moment. "You expect me to give the Historical Society veto power over the sale of the Quayside? We're only designating the restaurant as a heritage site, not the entire building." Were these people out of their minds? Nobody would put a caveat like that on a hundred-million-dollar asset. The shareholders would go ballistic.

"It's a standard contract," said Miriam.

"Standard for *whom?*" asked Derek, the tone revealing his incredulity.

"Standard for the Historical Society," said Myrna.

"I can't sign this," said Derek.

"But…" Candy made a sound for the very first time. He caught her anxious gaze. He was sorry she was disappointed, but this was ridiculous.

"It would be totally irresponsible," he pointed out, just in case she wasn't following the thread. "The asset would immediately lose market value, it would tie our hands…."

He flipped through a few more pages. "This contract designates the *entire* hotel as a heritage site. Do you have any idea how that would compromise Reeves-DuCarter's profitability position?"

Candy blinked, and her gaze went flat. "And we wouldn't want to do anything that would compromise our profitability position, would we?"

Oh, great. She was on *that* bandwagon again.

"I can't let the shareholders down," he insisted. Hell, they'd probably boot him off the Reeves-DuCarter board if he signed this document. They'd certainly be within their rights to revoke his vice presidency. Derek himself would draw and quarter any vice president who made a decision like this.

"But it's okay to let me down?" asked Candy.

"It's not the same—"

Candy stood up, swooping her briefcase off the table. "No. You're right. It's not the same thing, is it? How silly of me." She marched for the door.

Derek cursed under his breath. She didn't understand. If it were his building alone, if it were just *his* money at stake, he could take the risk. But his first loyalty was to the shareholders. It had to be.

CANDICE MARCHED down the hallway of the Historical Society offices and punched the elevator button. She wasn't worried about Derek coming after her. He'd shown her in no uncertain terms exactly where his loyalties lay.

Profit, profit, profit.

She stepped into the elevator.

How could she have ever imagined he was different? Why did she think for a minute she'd misjudged him? That he had a heart? That he had a soul?

Oh, it was all well and good to dabble in being a responsible citizen, until it cost him something. He'd justified the cash outlay for the heritage designation by balancing off the value of the advertising campaign. But as soon as the balance sheet moved to the good of society, he bailed.

He'd bailed on Seattle. He'd bailed on Canna Interiors. And he'd bailed on Candice.

The elevator stopped and the doors slid open.

She didn't want to think about which hurt more. Her mind flashed to the magic of last night, and she cringed, shaking away the memories. It had all been an illusion. The Derek she'd fallen for, the Derek she'd slept with, didn't exist.

When she made it to the lobby, she flung open the exit doors, hailed a cab and punched a number into her cell phone.

Jenna answered. "Hello."

"It's off," said Candice, her voice flat and unemotional.

"What's off?"

"The heritage designation. Derek found out it was going to be too expensive, and he backed out."

"Really?"

"Yes."

"I find that hard to—"

"Believe it. I just left the Historical Society's office. He's there right now explaining why he can't make the deal."

"But—"

"He's a fraud, Jenna. He strung me along while he thought there was profit in it, and then he cut me loose." Her voice cracked. "He's a shark. Just like all the rest of them. Why did I ever think he could be different?"

Candice closed her eyes. How could she have opened herself up to him? Opened her heart? Opened her soul? Handed him the ammunition to hurt her?

"I'm such a fool," she whispered half to herself.

"What happened between you two last night?" asked Jenna.

"Exactly what you think happened between us last night. We went back to his place. We made love. I slept in his arms all night long, and then he cut me off at the knees." Candice inhaled a shuddering breath. "Never again, Jenna."

"Don't let it—"

"*Never* again."

"Did you talk to him? Are you sure you didn't misunderstand?"

Candice let out a harsh laugh. "He said he couldn't let the shareholders down. So I reminded him that he was letting me down. He said, and I quote, 'It's not the same thing.'"

Jenna was silent for a beat. "Oh."

"Yeah. I gotta go. I just wanted to let you—"

"Let's meet for coffee."

"Maybe later."

"Candice."

"I'm fine. I just need some time alone."

"Where are you going?"

"Home, I guess." Somewhere safe to lick her wounds. Somewhere she could regroup. Losing the heritage designation was a professional setback, but she'd recover. She wasn't so sure about having lost her heart.

AS HE DROVE down Everett Street, convincing himself that Candy would get over it, strategizing about how to contact her and when to contact her, Derek's cell phone rang.

He pulled it out of his suit pocket. "Reeves here."

"Get your ass over here." It was Tyler's voice.

"What the hell—"

"I don't know what you did to Candice, but you've got Jenna cussing out your name and trashing the kitchen."

"It's a misunderstanding," said Derek.

"Well fix it! If you ever want to see Candice again, and if you ever want to speak with Jenna again, and if you don't want to shell out a million dollars for my kitchen, *fix your mess*."

"I had no choice," said Derek, even as the thought of never seeing Candy again hit him in the gut like a sucker punch. She wouldn't hold a grudge like that. Not forever.

Would she?

"There's always a choice," said Tyler.

"Did Jenna tell you what happened?"

"No. She's too busy spouting what you deserve— in frightening anatomical detail." Tyler's voice went up. "I don't want to know that my wife is capable of those thoughts. Do you understand me?"

"I was protecting the company," said Derek, getting sicker by the minute at the thought of never seeing Candy again. Tyler couldn't be right. He *couldn't* be right.

"You mean to tell me there wasn't a way to protect the company without screwing Candice and Jenna?"

"You shareholders, you're always quick enough to spend the profits, but then you want to sit back and be an armchair quarterback on the methods. I did it for you. *You*. If it was just my money…"

A few seconds ticked by while Derek's mind started to hum.

"What?" asked Tyler.

If it was just Derek's money, would he have picked the hotel over his relationship with Candy? Would he have compromised his own future financial interest for the good of Canna Interiors, for the good of Candy?

He groaned out loud. Would he have given up his vice presidency? His hotel? His money? Just to make Candy happy?

"What?" Tyler demanded again.

Yes! The money was nothing, and Candy was everything.

"Meet me at Reeves-DuCarter," said Derek. "In the boardroom."

"Now? On a Saturday?"

"Yes, *now*. I'm the vice president of the company and I'm calling an emergency meeting. You phone Striker. I'll phone Dad."

"But—"

"Do it."

Derek hit the End button and dialed his parents' house. He'd always prided himself on being a man of principles. And today he'd slammed headlong into one. Candy might never speak to him again, but he was going to fix what he'd broken.

DEREK STOOD AT THE HEAD of yet another boardroom table. This was a bigger boardroom, a bigger table, finer quality furniture because his company was so damn successful. For the very first time in his life he questioned the value of that success in something other than monetary terms.

The money was the easy part, he realized. It had always been the easy part.

He stared into the faces of his brothers, his parents and his two sisters-in-law. "Thank you all for coming on such short notice."

Tyler guffawed.

Jenna elbowed him in the ribs.

"I'd like to put a motion before the board," said Derek. "I'm resigning as vice president."

A collective gasp came up around the table, and his mother's eyes went wide.

"And I'm proposing a deal to sell my shares in Reeves-DuCarter—"

"Derek." His father stood up. "You're going to have to—"

Derek held up his hand. "Let me finish."

His father clamped his jaw shut as the room went still. As president and CEO, nobody *ever* interrupted Jackson at the boardroom table.

After a tense moment, he sat back down.

"I'm proposing a trade," said Derek. "Alfred Gray is working out the details right now. I want to give up my interest in Reeves-DuCarter in exchange for sole ownership of the Quayside."

"What?" asked his mother. "Where? Why?" She held up her hands in a gesture of confusion.

"I want to designate it as a heritage site. But that will compromise the market value, tie our hands on a future sale and a whole list of other issues. I can't ask the shareholders to take the risk."

Tyler spoke up. "But you're willing to take the risk yourself."

Derek nodded.

"And I thought I had it bad," Tyler muttered.

Jenna elbowed him again.

Striker shook his head and snickered. "So toast."

"We can't let you do that, son," said his father.

Derek's gaze flew to Jackson.

His father stood up and addressed the entire table. "All those in favor of letting Derek trade his shares?"

Nobody moved.

"All those opposed?"

Every hand went up.

Derek glared from one brother to the next, then to his father, as he frantically scrambled for a way to convince them.

Then Tyler spoke up. "All those in favor of designating the Quayside as a heritage site?"

All hands went up again.

Derek blinked. He took a step back and nearly stumbled. That made no sense. It was a foolish move. It was going to cost them all…

Jenna whispered something to Tyler and left the room.

Derek's mother beamed at him. "I think a heritage designation is an excellent idea."

Derek stared back. "But… It *will* cost you money."

"It's our civic duty," she said. "And I'm proud of you for recognizing it."

"Your mother is right," said his father. "I think Reeves-DuCarter ought to start building a higher community profile."

Derek shook his head. The excuses were all perfectly plausible, but they were doing this for him. He couldn't let them compromise their own interests.

"Let me sell my shares," he said, "buy the hotel. Alfred Gray will work up something fair."

"You were voted down," said his father.

"That's only because you're all trying—"

"To support you?" asked his mother. "I know you're used to being the family caretaker. And we appreciate your efforts, really, we do. But it's our turn to give back. There are many good reasons to approve the heritage designation."

Striker straightened. "So, shut up and start the paperwork, big brother."

Tyler chuckled. "And don't forget to say thank you."

Derek's shoulders slumped in complete amazement. He glanced from family member to family member. They really wanted to do this. They really wanted to help him.

"Thank you," he said, his voice raw.

THE THIRD TIME HER PHONE RANG, Candice picked it up. Whoever was on the other end, obviously wasn't going to leave a voice mail. "Yeah?"

"You'd better get over here," said Jenna.

"Over where?"

"The Reeves-DuCarter boardroom."

Candice's stomach plummeted. "No way."

"You won't *believe* what Derek did."

"I already know what Derek did."

"No you don't. He just tried to give it all up for you."

Candice frowned. "Give what up?"

"Everything. His life. His *empire*."

"Huh?"

"For *you*."

"What?"

"He stood there in front of his entire family and offered to trade them *all* of his shares in Reeves-DuCarter for sole interest in the Quayside."

Candice gave her head a little shake. "Why would he do that?"

"You can't think of a reason? You can't think of one reason why he might have wanted to own the Quayside?"

"No."

"To designate it as a heritage site."

Candice dropped down onto the sofa. Her throat went dry and her voice was barely a whisper. "What?"

Jenna's voice was chopped and static. "Get your butt over here."

Adrenaline shot through Candice's brain, shocking her out of her stupor. What was he doing? What did it mean?

She dropped the phone and grabbed her purse. He loved being vice president. He lived for the action, the excitement, the *deal.* He was a shark. Sharks didn't give up money and stature. Not for anything.

Skipping the elevator, she raced down the stairs of her apartment to the parking garage and peeled out onto the street.

When she arrived at the Reeves-DuCarter building, Jenna opened the front door, then grabbed an empty elevator.

"He loves you," said Jenna.

"Don't be ridiculous." Candice couldn't dare hope. Her broken heart was Derek's forever, but he had a million other things in his life. There had to be an explanation, and he'd darn well better get ready to give it to her.

The elevator doors slid open, and they rounded the corner and ran smack into Derek.

"Candy?"

Candice came to a stop in front of him, while Jenna discretely kept going.

"What are you doing?" she demanded.

"Coming to find you."

"Not that what." She gestured around the hallway. "I mean, *what* are you doing?"

The rest of Derek's family spilled out of the boardroom down the hall.

Derek grabbed Candice's arm and pulled her into an executive office, closing the door behind them. He looked into her eyes. "I really was coming to find you."

"Jenna said you sold your shares."

"If I did, would you care?"

"Of *course* I'd care."

"I thought money wasn't important to you?"

"But it's important to you. You can't give up your job, your life, your *dreams* to make me happy."

"Why not?"

"Because… *Derek*."

"Want to make a deal?"

Candice paused. "What kind of a deal?"

He moved toward her. "I'll get the Quayside designated as a heritage site, if you'll marry me and have my children."

"Your *children?*"

He took her hand. "Okay, just marry me. We can work out something on the children later."

Love swelled within her chest. "I can't let you do it."

"It's a win-win."

She shook her head.

"I love you, Candy."

She blinked away the burning sensation behind

her eyes. "I love you, too. But you can't give up your company."

He smiled. "Let me worry about the company. You want the heritage designation? You'll have to marry me. I'm not above playing hardball, Candy."

"Neither am I," she said softly. "I'll marry you if you keep your shares in Reeves-DuCarter."

"Deal." He leaned forward and kissed her.

She pulled back. "Just like that."

He nodded and kissed her again. This time the kiss was longer, deeper, soul-satisfying. Derek loved her. And they were staying together. Forever.

The heritage designation was nothing.

The office door opened, but she couldn't quite bring herself to break the kiss. Derek kept kissing her until his father cleared his throat.

They both looked up.

"Your mother's asking if she should get out Grandma's rings?" He cocked his head sideways and smiled. "I'm assuming it's a yes?"

Derek nodded. "Looks like we've made ourselves a deal."

"You promised not to give up your shares," Candice reminded Derek, making sure his father over-heard. She wanted to put a stop to this before any paperwork changed hands.

"He's not giving up his shares," said his father.

Candice blinked.

"We voted that idea down immediately."

She slanted a suspicious gaze at Derek.

He gave her a squeeze and a wicked smile. "But we're getting the heritage designation anyway. Isn't it great?"

"You tricked me?"

"Gotta stay on your toes around me, babe."

ALTHOUGH THE WEDDING wasn't officially a heritage event, Candice's gown was vintage flocked satin with shimmering lace insets. It had been worn by Derek's grandmother in 1943—the wonderful woman who had also worn the engagement and wedding rings that now adorned Candice's left hand.

Candice had never pictured herself having a formal wedding. But now she felt like a fairy princess, floating around the Quayside dance floor in Derek's arms with all the eyes in the room on her. She wiggled her ring finger in front of her eyes, watching the diamonds sparkle under the ballroom lights.

"I can't believe we're married," she sighed.

"I can't believe I'm having so much fun," said Derek.

Candice looked up. "Excuse me?"

He gathered her closer. "When my brothers got married, all I could see was that they were tossing away their freedom."

She smiled. "And now you've tossed yours away, too."

"But it doesn't work that way."

"Sorry, buddy, but the deal's done. Your freedom's gone."

Derek chuckled. "I mean, the engagement, the

wedding, the marriage, it's not about *my* freedom. It's all about keeping the woman I love so close to me that she'll never get away."

"I don't want to get away."

"That's good." He gently kissed her forehead. "Because the deal's done for you, too. You're mine for life."

The band switched songs and the wedding party joined them on the dance floor, Jenna and Erin in their deep blue bridesmaids dresses, and Tyler and Striker in their tuxedos.

Her parents danced along beside them, giving her smiles and whispered congratulations.

"Going to throw the bouquet?" asked Erin as she whirled by with Striker.

"Following right in your footsteps," said Candice.

Striker grinned and winked at his wife. "Then I hope you're planning a family soon." He cupped his palm over Erin's abdomen.

Candice's eyes widened. "Really?"

Erin nodded.

"Congratulations," said Derek. "Does Mom know?"

"We're saving the news until after your honeymoon," said Striker.

"Maybe I *won't* throw the bouquet after all," said Candice.

Erin laughed as they danced away.

"That's right," Derek drawled. "We haven't had our children negotiation yet."

Candice tipped her head back. "Okay. What are you offering?"

"Two girls for two boys?"

"*Four?*"

"Not enough?"

"Get real."

"How about if we start with one and take it from there?"

"Right away?" Candice wasn't sure if she was ready to be a mother. But she definitely wanted Derek's children.

He shook his head. "Doesn't have to be right away. But, I warn you, my mother *will* start lobbying...."

Tyler and Jenna danced closer.

"Finally a groom," said Tyler with a wide grin. "How the mighty have fallen."

"Yeah, yeah," said Derek. "I know. You told me so. So when are you guys having kids?"

Jenna paled.

"What?" asked Candice, worried.

"How did you know?" asked Jenna.

"Know?" asked Candice. Then her eyes widened. "You're *not*."

Jenna's face broke into a sheepish grin. "We are."

"Does Mom know?" asked Derek.

"We're waiting until after your honeymoon."

"Congratulations," said Derek and Candice simultaneously as Tyler and Jenna danced away.

"Well," said Candice, settling comfortably into Derek's arms. "Guess that'll take the pressure off us."

"And here I was thinking, 'if you can't beat 'em...'"

"You in a hurry?" asked Candice.

"Nah. Not really. Well, maybe."

"You're not going to sic your mother on me, are you? Because only a wussie gets his mommy to help him make a deal."

Derek leaned in, giving her a lingering kiss on the neck, followed by another kiss on her collarbone, then yet another one lightly on the tip of her shoulder.

Candice sighed, melting against him again. "How long before we can cut out on this crowd?"

She felt him smile.

"See," he said. "I don't need my mommy. I have complete faith in my own powers of persuasion."

"You forget, I got the carpet *and* the chandelier."

"But you married me in the end."

Candice held up her left hand. "Small price to pay. I got the antique rings."

"You mean this whole thing was a conspiracy to get the rings?"

Candice grinned. "Gotta stay on your toes around me, babe."

* * * * *

*Look for Barbara Dunlop
next in Silhouette Desire!*

Harlequin on Location

hot tips

Wherever your dream date location,
pick a setting and a time that won't be
interrupted by your daily responsibilities.
This is a special time together. Here are
a few hopelessly romantic settings to
inspire you—they might as well be ripped
right out of a Harlequin romance novel!

Bad weather can be so good.

Take a walk together after a fresh snowfall or when it's just stopped raining. Pick a snowball (or a puddle) fight, and see how long it takes to get each other soaked to the bone. Then enjoy drying off in front of a fire, or perhaps surrounded by lots and lots of candles with yummy hot chocolate to warm things up.

Candlelight dinner for two...in the bedroom.

Romantic music and candles will instantly transform the place you sleep into a cozy little love nest, perfect for nibbling. Why not lay down a blanket and open a picnic basket at the foot of your bed? Or set a beautiful table with your finest dishes and glowing candles to set the mood. Either way, a little bubbly and lots of light finger foods will make this a meal to remember.

A Wild and Crazy Weeknight.

Do something unpredictable...on a weeknight straight from work. Go to an art opening, a farm-team baseball game, the local playhouse, a book signing by an author or a jazz club—anything but the humdrum blockbuster movie. There's something very romantic about being a little wild and crazy—or at least out of the ordinary—that will bring out the flirt in both of you. And you won't be able to resist thinking about each other in anticipation of your hot date...or telling everyone the day after.

Are you a ♥ chocolate lover?

Try WALDORF ♥ ♥ CHOCOLATE FONDUE— a true chocolate decadence

hot tips

While many couples choose to dine out on Valentine's Day, one of the most romantic things you can do for your sweetheart is to prepare an elegant meal—right in the comfort of your own home.

Harlequin asked John Doherty, executive chef at the Waldorf-Astoria Hotel in New York City, for his recipe for seduction—the famous Waldorf Chocolate Fondue....

WALDORF CHOCOLATE FONDUE
Serves 6-8

2 cups water
½ cup corn syrup
1 cup sugar
8 oz dark bitter chocolate, chopped
1 pound cake (can be purchased in supermarket)
2–3 cups assorted berries
2 cups pineapple
½ cup peanut brittle

Bring water, corn syrup and sugar to a boil in a medium-size pot. Turn off the heat and add the chopped chocolate. Strain and pour into fondue pot. Cut cake and fruit into cubes and 1-inch pieces. Place fondue pot in the center of a serving plate, arrange cake, fruit and peanut brittle around pot. Serve with forks.

Looking for a seductive cocktail?

hot tips

Try *Ero-Desiac*—
a dazzling martini

With its warm apricot walls yet cool atmosphere, Verlaine is quickly becoming one of New York's hottest nightspots. Verlaine created a light, subtle yet seductive martini for Harlequin: the Ero-Desiac. Sake warms the heart and soul, while jasmine and passion fruit ignite the senses....

The Ero-Desiac

Combine vodka, sake, passion fruit puree and jasmine tea. Mix and shake. Strain into a martini glass, then rest pomegranate syrup on the edge of the martini glass and drizzle the syrup down the inside of the glass.

If you enjoyed what you just read,
then we've got an offer you can't resist!

Take 2 bestselling love stories FREE!

Plus get a FREE surprise gift!

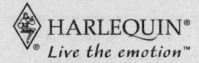